SCENT OF PERIL

A CHRISTIAN ROMANTIC SUSPENSE

SULLIVAN K9 SEARCH AND RESCUE

LAURA SCOTT

1

Jessica Sullivan frowned when she spied Logan Fletcher's plane making a wide arc above the ranch. Logan hadn't mentioned stopping by, so she wasn't sure what had brought him to their neck of the woods. Since losing their parents five and a half years ago, she lived on the Sullivan K9 Search and Rescue Ranch with her eight siblings. They'd turned the family's former lush dude ranch into a renowned search and rescue operation.

Eyeing Logan's plane, she had to acknowledge her feelings toward Logan were—complicated. She'd had a crush on him in high school—while he'd been dating her best friend, Ella. Then Ella had died of a drug overdose. Losing her friend had killed her crush, as Jess had held Logan responsible.

But he'd claimed he wasn't involved. That he'd never done drugs and hadn't even known Ella had started using them. Ella's brother, Ethan, had also blamed Logan. Eight years later, she'd managed to forgive him to a point. But their once close relationship had been lost forever.

With a sigh, she glanced down at her K9, Teddy, a black Belgian sheepdog that had been trained as a narcotics dog. She'd worked for the TSA prior to her parents' death. Since returning to the ranch, she'd begun cross-training Teddy on people scents to help their search and rescue operations. She might be biased, but Teddy was a quick learner. Eager to please, unlike Chase's K9, Rocky. Spring was in the air, but there was still plenty of snow on the ground. Logan would land his prop plane on the makeshift air landing strip they kept plowed year-round specifically for this purpose. When it came to search and rescue, they never knew what method of travel they'd need to use.

"Come, Teddy." She turned her back on her three-bedroom cabin to trudge across the ranch yard. As she approached the airstrip, she watched Logan land the plane with grace and skill. She had flown with him several times, along with Teddy, making sure her K9 wore earphones to protect his ears. She trusted Logan's piloting skills. Standing off to the side with her dog, she waited for Logan to jump down from behind the pilot's seat.

"Jess!" He jogged toward her. "I'm glad you're here."

"I live here," she said dryly. When he flushed, she waved a hand. "Sorry, I didn't mean to sound sarcastic. What's going on?"

"I was flying near the Bighorn Mountains earlier when I spotted what appears to be a piece of a tail fin from a plane." His green eyes locked on hers. "I immediately thought of you. I think we should head over to check it out."

A piece from her parents' plane? Her heart thumped in her chest. Five and a half years ago, she and her siblings had scoured the mountainside searching for their parents and the plane without success. As it happened, her parents were flying with a friend who had not installed a black box, which would have helped them locate the wreckage. "Where exactly did you spot it?"

"Easier if I show you." At her look of impatience, Logan shrugged. "To be honest, it's several miles from the projected path of your parents' route, so it's not within the usual search zone. But I circled around twice to log the location before heading here."

That made her frown. "It could be from any plane."

"Maybe." He agreed. "I still think it's worth checking out."

"Okay. Let me grab Teddy's gear." She didn't want to leave her K9 behind. "I'll make a few sandwiches too."

"That sounds good. I'll wait here." Logan gestured to his plane. "I'll do a quick maintenance check."

Jess knew Logan took his charter flying business seriously. He was more than the pilot; he performed all the maintenance work on his three different planes himself. She appreciated the extra safety precautions.

Despite losing her parents to a small plane crash, she wasn't afraid of flying. Thankfully, Teddy didn't mind flying either.

Returning to her cabin, she threw extra dog food, water, and K9 protective gear into a duffel. She took a few minutes to slap a couple of thick ham sandwiches together and packed them along with some additional items in a smaller backpack for herself. She already wore all-terrain boots but swapped out her regular hat and gloves for woolen ones. The weather was mild now, but it was better to be prepared.

"Come, Teddy." As she turned to head back outside, she debated letting Maya or Chase know her plans. Then she decided against it. There would be plenty of time to fill them in if they were able to find and retrieve the plane debris.

If she and Logan couldn't find it, there was no sense in getting her older siblings' hopes up. As a family, they'd come to grips with their loss. Their faith in God and in knowing their parents had everlasting life with Jesus helped. It was the not knowing what had happened or why their parents' plane had crashed that hurt the most.

A mystery that remained unsolved all these years later.

She quickened her pace with the backpack snug over her shoulders and the duffel thumping along her side. Teddy trotted next to her, his snout in the air. Even when he wasn't working, Teddy eagerly explored his surroundings with his nose.

Logan stepped back from the plane, then crossed over to take the duffel from her. "I'll store this in the back. Go ahead and jump in."

This was a routine they'd done often, but Teddy's ears pricked forward as he sniffed the passenger seat of the plane. Then he abruptly sat and let out a sharp bark.

What in the world? That was Teddy's alert for scenting drugs.

She took a step back, wondering if something else had caught the K9's attention. Logan was still storing the duffel in the back, so she held Teddy's gaze. "Search! Search for peppers!" Peppers was the word she used for drugs. She didn't like calling them candy, the way some narcotics handlers did. She personally hated peppers, so that was the term she'd used for drugs, which she also despised. It seemed the most appropriate for working with Teddy.

Teddy jumped to all fours and sniffed the area around the plane again. Then in almost the exact same spot, he sat and let out a sharp bark.

"What's up with Teddy?" Logan asked.

She whirled to face him. "You tell me. He's alerting on drugs. Drugs, Logan. Since when do you transport drugs?"

"What are you talking about?" Logan reared back as if she'd slapped him. "I have never transported drugs."

"Wrong answer." She gestured toward Teddy. "Teddy alerted on the scent of drugs."

Logan frowned, then rushed forward to look around the interior of his plane. She stayed back, not sure she was ready to go anywhere with him.

Then he turned, his expression grim as he held up a black glove. "My last charter passenger must have left this behind."

She walked forward to see it for herself. "You're saying that guy may have been carrying drugs?"

Logan glanced at Teddy. "Your dog seems to

think so. That's the reason I was up over the mountains in the first place. I dropped this guy off at a small landing area that wasn't too far away from the location where I spotted the tail fin. It's not like I search people who pay for transportation. He didn't appear to be under the influence or anything."

"Where did he come from?"

"Cheyenne." Logan frowned. "I have his name written down, but he paid in cash."

Her eyes narrowed. "And you didn't find that suspicious?"

A flash of anger darkened his eyes. "No, I didn't. Those who can afford to charter a private plane often pay in cash. There's no crime in hiring a plane. Doug paid me in cash back in January when he needed help. This is my business, remember? Besides, as I said, he seemed okay. Had a bunch of hunting and fishing gear."

"Hunting in April?" she scoffed. "Not likely."

"Wild turkey hunting is legal in April," Logan said. "And fly-fishing opens in April. Look, it's not my job to quiz these guys on their plans. He paid for a plane ride, and I flew him to his destination. End of story."

"Except it's not the end of the story," she shot back. "Teddy alerted on drugs. That means your guy could be up to no good."

Logan sighed and rubbed the back of his neck.

"I know that now. What do you want me to do? Call the local police?"

She thought about that for a moment. They could alert her brother-in-law, Doug Bridges, about their suspicions. Doug was a former DEA agent who now worked for the Wyoming State Department of Criminal Investigations. The other option was to alert the game warden for the area. His name was Eddie Marsh.

"Jess, we don't know this guy is a criminal," Logan said. "He could have a legit prescription for pain meds. Or maybe he was carrying a small stash of weed."

"You're right." She knew she was overreacting. Maybe because of the way Ella had overdosed all those years ago. She hated the idea of drugs being so accessible. But Ella had made the decision to take them. A choice that had proven fatal. Jess shook off the depression. "Okay fine. Let's go. But I hope you don't hear from that guy again. He may have a legit prescription, or he may not. This could be some new way of transporting drugs from one area of the state to the next."

Logan hesitated, then nodded. "I agree. I'll be too busy to take him on another trip."

A flash of guilt hit hard. This was Logan's livelihood. She had no right to ask him to turn down paying clients. Especially not during the colder months of the year when there were fewer tourists flocking to the area.

Still, turkey hunting and fly-fishing in April seemed a stretch. Spring might be in the air, warming the daytime temperatures to a balmy forty to fifty degrees, but during the night the temps dropped like a rock.

"Are you ready?" Logan sounded impatient.

"Yes. Get in, Teddy." She waved to the plane. She decided against rewarding her K9 for his alert since there was no way to prove the dog had actually scented drugs. After the dog gracefully jumped into the plane, she followed suit.

But as Logan went through his checklist for takeoff, she made a note to let Doug know about Teddy's alert when they returned. Better to play it safe.

Especially if the guy was up to no good.

LOGAN STARTED THE PLANE ENGINE, glancing at Teddy who wore earmuffs like a pro. He'd seen the Sullivan K9s in action on many occasions, but this was the first time he'd been on the receiving end of an alert.

Had Craig Benton, his last charter client, been transporting drugs? At the time, the guy hadn't seemed like someone who would be involved in that sort of thing. But now he kept seeing the roll of cash the guy had pulled from his pocket. Benton had peeled ten crisp one-hundred-dollar bills from the roll, handing them over without hesitation.

A drug dealer? Or just a rich guy looking to spend time in the mountains?

He turned his attention to flying the plane. He radioed the closest tower, located at Yellowstone Airport, to confirm his flight plan.

"Roger, two-five-seven, you're good to go," the dispatcher said.

"Ten-four," he responded. Sensing Jessica's gaze, he glanced over. "What?"

"Nothing. It's just that every time we fly, I think of my parents heading home from Billings." She waved a hand toward the Bighorn Mountains looming ahead. "I still don't understand why they crashed."

He thought about the jagged section of a tail fin he'd glimpsed from the sky. If he hadn't taken Craig Benton to meet his alleged hunting buddies at the base of the mountain, he wouldn't have seen it. "I'm sure it's not easy to move forward without answers."

She nodded without saying anything. He might wish things could be different between him and Jess, but Ella's death loomed large between them. For the hundredth time, he wished he'd never asked

Ella out. That he'd never gotten involved with the prettiest girl in their high school class in the first place.

But he had. And his life had been forever changed by her death.

Jess hadn't been the only one who'd stared at him with accusing eyes. Ella's brother, Ethan, had been extremely vocal. The local sheriff's department had executed a search warrant on his house, his car, and his plane. They hadn't found any drugs, but most of the townsfolk had assumed he'd gotten rid of the evidence.

Eventually, the whispers had stopped. But he knew there were still people in Cody who blamed him for Ella's death.

Like Jess. Oh, she'd claimed that was nothing more than ancient history, but the old feelings had resurfaced after Teddy had alerted on the scent of drugs in his plane. The way she'd glared at him with suspicion had struck deep in his core.

He banked the Cessna to the right. Jessica leaned forward, searching the ground below. "We're still ten minutes from the general area," he told her.

She nodded to indicate she'd heard but continued scanning the rocky terrain below. No doubt, she was hoping to spot additional debris.

He understood her desire for answers. Five years ago, he'd logged countless flight hours while searching for her parents' plane. Chase had insisted on paying for his fuel and time, and he'd only accepted because he'd been forced to turn away paying jobs in order to continue making flights to the mountainside and back. Something he wouldn't have been able to do without the additional financial help.

The entire Sullivan family had been very grateful for his efforts. Even Jess.

He'd have given anything to have found something useful back then. And he had never stopped searching during his flights.

He found himself hoping this bit of plane debris would bring some answers.

Using the landmark of a jagged rock poking out from the side of the mountain, he slowly dropped the plane's altitude. Tracking the rocky outcropping, he turned twenty degrees, then peered down through his side window.

"There it is!" He couldn't hide his excitement. "Do you see it?"

"I think so." Jess's voice was uncertain. "I mean, I see something white, but I can't tell what it is from here."

"Hang on, I'll circle around so we can get a little lower." He banked the plane in an arc, putting some distance between the plane and the trees leering upward from the mountain.

He took the Cessna down another few hundred feet. This was the best he could do without risking the tops of some of the tree branches scraping along the underbelly of the plane.

"I think you're right," Jess said. "I can tell that it looks like the tail of a plane."

"I'll see if I can find a place to land." He knew without being told that Jess wanted to retrieve the piece of debris. "It will be a long hike."

"I know, but we have plenty of daylight left." She glanced at him. "It's only noon. We'll eat our lunch and head out. We should be able to get there and back to the plane in plenty of time."

"Okay." He knew the mountains could be deceptive when it came to distance. What looked like an hour-long hike was likely triple that time frame. Especially since there was still plenty of snow covering the ground.

But this was why he'd brought her to the area, so there was no point in complaining. Thankfully, he always carried plenty of winter-weather gear. He wasn't nearly as worried about the elements as he was about potentially damaging his plane. He scanned the area below. "Help me spot an area to land."

Jess was silent for a moment. He noticed the long, flat stretch of land at the same time she did. "How about there?"

"It could be private property." It seemed as if the stretch of land had been used as a landing strip in the past, as it was cleared of snow and brush. It wasn't the one he'd used to drop off Craig Benton, but it wasn't that far away either. He didn't see a sign of a dwelling nearby. After a moment's hesitation, he shrugged. "Okay, that will work. Hang on."

Jess nodded. She wasn't a nervous flier, taking the usual air-pocket bumps in stride. He turned again so he could approach the strip of open land straight on, then brought the plane in for a landing.

The minute he brought the Cessna to a stop, Jess ripped her headphones off and turned to remove the headgear from her dog. He shouldn't have been surprised at how Teddy seemed to enjoy flying as much as Jess did.

"Down, Teddy." Jess jumped down from the plane. Her dog followed suit. Then she snagged her backpack and pulled out two thick sandwiches. "Here you go."

"Thanks." He gratefully took the sandwich. "We'll need to make sure we gear up," he said between bites. The weather in spring could be dicey. There were no storms in the forecast earlier, but that could easily change without warning. "We need to be prepared for anything."

"I know. That's why I brought my backpack and Teddy's duffel." She ate her sandwich, too, while rummaging in the duffel for her dog's equipment. The Sullivans always cared for their dogs before themselves.

After Jess finished eating, she placed a vest over Teddy's torso and added padded booties over his paws. Logan checked his own pack, taking note of the bottles of water, protein bars, and dried fruit and nut packs that would have to serve as a late snack or early dinner if needed. When Jess had finished with Teddy, who surprisingly didn't seem to mind the booties, he handed her half his rations. "We may need these later."

"Thank you." Her smile made his pulse jump. He forced himself to ignore the response. He was the last person Jess would consider dating, and the sooner he came to grips with that fact, the better.

"Anytime." They took a moment to tuck the supplies away before donning their thick outer gear. Jess stuffed some dog food into her backpack. They each had a pack, so he couldn't carry hers. "I have room if you need more supplies."

"This should be fine." She bent to give her dog some water from a collapsible dish. Then she straightened and tucked the dish into the pack. "Okay, we're ready."

"Let's do this." He headed off across the open stretch of land toward the woods surrounding the base of the mountain. Double-checking his compass, he verified they were headed in the correct direction.

Teddy navigated the rugged terrain without difficulty. He and Jess took things more slowly. It wasn't just the snow-covered rocks and fallen branches, but there was no distinct path for them to follow. They had to forge their own way, often through thick brush.

They didn't talk much, conserving their strength for the hike. After about forty minutes, Jess lifted her hand. "I'd like to give Teddy a break."

"I need it more than he does," he joked, sitting on a fallen log. Jess dropped beside him.

"Me too. I haven't given Teddy the search command to track anything, but the way he's sniffing around, I'm sure he's burning as much energy as if he were on the hunt."

Teddy sat beside her, looking up at her adoringly. The dog was protective of her, but thankfully, he didn't view Logan as a threat.

He checked his compass. Years of flying had honed his sense of direction, and he could easily picture the area where they'd spied the plane piece in his mind. "We're on the right trajectory. But we still have a good three miles to go."

"Okay." She took a sip of water, then passed the bottle to him. "That shouldn't be a problem."

He didn't doubt her ability to keep up. Over the

five years that the Sullivan family had been working search and rescue, he'd noticed they'd gotten in prime physical shape. He'd been so shallow in high school, far too concerned with dating the pretty, popular girl, that he'd overlooked the sweet and kind Jessica.

Reminding himself there was no point in re-living the past, he tucked the water bottle into his backpack, then stood and stretched. "Ready?"

"Yes." She rose to her feet. "Come, Teddy."

As if the dog wouldn't follow, he thought with a wry smile. With his black coat and protective na-ture, Teddy's name should have been Shadow.

They hiked for another thirty minutes, mostly in silence. Their conversation consisted of warning each other about environmental hazards such as fallen logs or the sudden appearance of a creek. Teddy forged ahead, then turned to wait for them to catch up before bounding forward again.

"He acts as if he knows our final destination," Logan said.

"I've noticed that too." She tracked the dog with her gaze. "Maybe he's just glad to be out in the wilderness."

He nodded. Jess would know her dog better than he did.

They stopped for another break. Once more, he looked down at his compass. "We're making good time," he said. "I estimate we have another thirty to forty minutes to go."

She gave her dog some water, then tipped her head back to gaze up at the sky. "As much as I hate daylight savings time, it's nice to know we have several hours of sunlight left."

He grunted in agreement.

After a ten-minute rest, they continued moving through the brush. He broke through a particularly dense section of woods to find the clearing.

"I don't remember seeing this from the plane," Jess said with a frown. "Do you?"

"Not really." He pulled out his compass to verify their location. "We may have veered slightly off course to the south. We'll need to turn north, up the slope."

"Okay." She flashed a grin. "At least heading back to the plane should be easier."

He took the lead, noticing that Teddy stayed closer to Jessica's side now. He didn't see any people tracks in the snow, so he didn't anticipate danger from a human perspective.

Wild animals were another story.

He made another correction in their path, then continued climbing. When he crested a hill, he stopped and swung his gaze to the right.

"I see it!" Quickening his pace, he slipped and slid on the snow toward the metal object that was larger here than he'd anticipated. He bent and picked up the large chunk of metal that was clearly from a small plane.

"Are there any markings on it?" Jess was breathless as she joined him. Teddy, too, sniffed at the metal with interest.

He carefully turned the tail fin in his hands. "No, I don't see any markings. Other than the rust from being in the elements."

Jess frowned. "So we really can't say for sure that this is a part of my parents' plane."

"No, we can't. But we can have it tested. Maybe there's a forensic way to identify how long this has been lying here."

"I like that idea." Jess's blue eyes filled with hope. "I'm so glad we came."

He was too. Anything for her to look at him like that.

A crack of gunfire rang out. Dropping the tail fin, Logan grabbed Jess's arm, pulling her toward the closest tree. But she jerked free to turn toward her dog. "Teddy, come!"

The dog ran toward her as another shot rang out, striking the tree not far from Jess. She threw herself over Teddy, hauling the dog behind the tree. Logan covered Jess's body with his, his mind racing. That last bullet had been too close for comfort.

Whoever was shooting at them wasn't hunting for wild turkeys.

Was this about his recent charter? Or something else?

Logan could only hope they'd survive long enough to find out.

2

____

Who was shooting at them? Jess huddled between Logan and Teddy, sweeping her gaze over the landscape. Two shots fired, but now there was nothing but silence.

"What's going on?" She peered up at Logan. He was close, covering her body with his. She was touched by his protective gesture. "Did you see anything?"

"No. I only heard the shots." Logan's expression was grim. "I think they're from a rifle, not a handgun."

She frowned. "How do you know?"

"It's a guess." He grimaced. "The gunshots weren't as loud as they would be if fired from a handgun at close range."

"A hunter?" She found that hard to believe.

"No. I don't think any hunter would be stupid enough to fire at two people. The bullet struck a tree branch over our heads." There was a pause, then he lifted his chin to the right. "I think the shots came from that ridge up there."

She quickly scanned the ridge but didn't see anything. "Are you sure?"

"Not for certain. See that outcropping of rock? That would be a good position for someone to use for a rifle shot."

"I could ask Teddy to search for gold," she said.

"Gold?" He frowned.

"Maya has encouraged us to cross-train our dogs for other scents. We use the term gold to identify gunpowder and gun oil," she explained. "Teddy has a good nose. I'm sure he'd be able to locate the bullet."

"That's not necessary. I don't think the bullet will tell us much. Besides, it could have gone another hundred yards before stopping. No sense risking our lives by sticking around for much longer." He straightened and lightly rested his hand on the center of her back. "Stay here with Teddy while I check it out."

"No, don't." She grasped his arm to prevent him from leaving. "As you pointed out, there's no reason to stay here. If that outcropping along the ridge is where the shooter had been standing, then we need to get out of here. I don't want to leave the metal part of the plane behind, though. We need to take that along with us."

He hesitated, his gaze sweeping the ridge. Then after a long moment, he nodded. "You're right. It's smarter for us to head back down the mountain. But we need to stay in the trees as much as possible."

No argument from her on that plan. "Give me a minute to grab the piece of plane we found."

"I'll do it." Before she could protest, he darted out into the clearing. Snagging the plane part up from the ground, he spun and ran back to the cover provided by the trees.

"It's bigger than I thought," she confessed. "Do you think it will fit in one of our backpacks?"

"Oh yeah." He shrugged out of the pack and began rearranging the items inside. She held the tail fin in her hand, examining it again more closely. There was plenty of rust, but no markings. She'd hoped that finding this would help them identify if the part came from her parents' plane.

But in all honesty, it could be from any plane. Who knew how many small planes were lost in the mountains each year.

Probably more than she wanted to know.

Logan took the piece of metal from her hands and tucked it into the backpack upside down. The broader base of the tail fin wouldn't fit inside the pack, but he wedged the smaller end inside as far as it could go, zipping the sides up as much as possible to keep it in place. He nodded and glanced up at her. "This should work."

"I agree." She was glad they wouldn't have to leave it behind. "Do you want me to carry that pack?"

"No, you have your own. I've got this." He glanced up at the ridge again, then stood and shouldered the pack. She hoped the extra weight wouldn't be a problem. "We need to move. You go first with Teddy. I'll cover our backs. The sooner we get down the slope, the better. I don't want to run across this guy up close and personal."

Jess didn't want that either. She slowly rose to a crouch, then did a quick examination of her dog to make sure he wasn't injured. He was fine. "Come, Teddy."

The dog looked up at her, then quickly followed her out from the shelter of the trees. The tiny hairs on the back of her neck rose in alarm as she took the lead in retracing their steps back down the mountain. Jess found herself hunching her shoulders, anticipating another attack. But after a solid ten minutes of walking, she slowly began to relax. There was nothing to worry about. They were already making good time heading back to the plane.

Maybe the shooter had been a hunter. A really bad hunter.

Logan stayed behind her. She glanced over her shoulder to check on him. He offered a reassuring smile. "You're doing great. Just keep following our original tracks down and to the east."

"Down is easy," she said lightly. That wasn't necessarily true. Her footing slipped in the snow more often than she liked, forcing her to grab at various branches along the way to keep herself upright. She was glad to have their previous footprints to use as a guide. The tracks should lead them back to where they'd started.

Teddy wasn't having any trouble navigating the terrain. All their search and rescue dogs were athletic and comfortable moving through the woods. Teddy glanced up at her often, staying close to her side. He wasn't a hunting dog, but the loud crack of gunfire was more than enough for him to identify a potential threat. If the shooter had been closer, Teddy would likely have alerted on his scent and growled in warning.

More proof that the shooter had purposefully stayed far away. Logan was right about the guy using a rifle.

After forty minutes, Logan called a halt. "Let's take a break."

She nodded and stopped near a group of pine

trees. This wasn't the spot where they'd previously taken a break, but it would do for now. She knew Logan was anxious to get back to the clearing where they'd left his plane. "No sign of anyone following?"

"Not that I can tell." Logan glanced at Teddy. "Your dog didn't seem to notice anything off either."

"I guess that's a good thing." She sat on a stump, gratefully accepting a sip of water from Logan. Then she poured some water into a collapsible bowl for Teddy. "I don't understand why anyone would shoot at us."

Logan's expression hardened. "I have one possible theory."

"Like what?"

"My charter client claimed he was here to do hunting and fishing. I dropped him off at a location that isn't that far from here. That's how I spied the piece of plane debris." He made a circle in the air with a gloved hand. "Because I was here in this area."

She wasn't following. "And you think that guy may have been the shooter?"

"Him or one of his cronies." Logan glanced at Teddy again. "Your K9 alerted to the scent of drugs in my plane where Craig Benton dropped his glove. Now that we've been targeted by gunfire, I'm less likely to believe he had a legitimate prescription for narcotics."

Realization dawned. "You think he is involved in drug trafficking. And he fired those shots to drive us away."

"Exactly." Logan shook his head. "I don't like the idea of being hired by guys like Benton to bring drugs in and out of the area."

"I don't either." She swallowed hard, considering his theory. "We need to call the local sheriff's department and the game warden. They'll need to head back to that area to see if they can find that guy. What's his name? Craig Benton?"

"That's the name he gave me." Logan grimaced. "Like I said, he paid in cash. If he's involved in drugs, I doubt he used his real name."

"You're right; he probably didn't." She stroked Teddy's soft ears. "Maybe we should turn around and head back. See if Teddy alerts on anything."

"No way." Logan's tone was sharp. "Too dangerous."

With a sigh, she nodded. He was right. She wouldn't risk her dog without having more backup. "Okay, I get it. Neither of us is armed. I can bring Teddy back with the local authorities later."

He scowled. "Still too dangerous."

"Maybe." She knew her brothers would share his opinion. "But Teddy is the expert when it comes to finding drugs. And if that's what's going on here, then he's our best chance at discovering where they may be hidden."

There was a long moment of silence as Logan stared at her. She stared back, unwilling to back down. Finally, he rose to his feet. "Let's keep going. The sooner we get back to civilization, the better."

She nodded and stood. Logan hung back, clearly expecting her to continue taking the lead. "Come, Teddy."

They walked in silence. Mostly because that made it easier to hear anything unusual, but also because Logan was not happy about her plan to return with Teddy.

Her thoughts went back to the rusted plane part they'd found. Her oldest sister, Maya, had married Doug Bridges a month ago, but they'd delayed their honeymoon until after Chase and Wynona's wedding. Doug and Maya were spending a week in Hawaii on their honeymoon but were due to head back to the ranch today. Doug was a former federal agent who currently worked for the CDI, Criminal Division of Investigations for the state of Wyoming. She had no doubt her brother-in-law would know who to contact about testing the chunk of rusted metal to see if it could have come from their parents' plane.

And if not? No, she wasn't going to think about that possibility. Sure, the location was miles from where they'd originally searched. That search had been done according to the original flight plan. But who knows what really happened that fateful day.

She and her siblings had waited five years, and counting, without getting answers related to the plane crash that killed their parents.

If this piece of tail fin was from their plane, then she knew the entire Sullivan crew and their respective K9s would head back out to search the area.

But they couldn't do that, she realized grimly, if a shooter was hanging around.

Jess was so lost in her thoughts she tripped over a branch, nearly tumbling to the ground. She caught herself in time, then frowned. "Logan?"

"What is it?" He was at her side in a heartbeat. "Are you hurt?"

"No, I'm fine." She'd twisted her ankle a bit, but it wasn't serious. She gestured to the left. "Do you see the tracks?"

He followed her gloved hand, his expression going hard. "I don't remember seeing those on the way up."

"I didn't notice them either." She grimaced. "Although to be fair, I wasn't really looking for anything like that." The footprints seemed to lead the opposite direction.

"Stay here." Without waiting for her to reply, Logan veered off their path to cut over to the new set of footprints. She watched as he crouched down to examine them more closely. Then he stood and looked around. "They look relatively recent, maybe from earlier today even. And they're heading away from the area where we found the tail fin."

The knot of tension in her stomach loosened. "So probably not the shooter."

"Probably not." He didn't appear convinced. After another long moment, he turned and hurried back to where she was waiting. "Either way, I think we need to get out of here."

"I'm with you on that." She pushed forward, following their earlier tracks. But as they walked, she couldn't help glancing over her shoulder, hoping and praying that whoever left those tracks wasn't hiding back there, watching them.

LOGAN DIDN'T LIKE any of this one bit. And it grated on his nerves to know that it had been his bright idea to come here today. To locate and retrieve the piece of tail that was currently sticking up out of his backpack.

Not that he could have anticipated someone shooting at them. He had a sidearm in his plane. He should have grabbed it for their hike. A handgun didn't have the range of a rifle, but it was better than nothing.

He hated knowing this was just the beginning. Of course, Jess would offer to return to the area with Teddy to see if they could find drugs. Or the gunman.

If not for the idiot taking potshots at them, he'd have taken the time to spread out and search for more plane debris. He knew Jess and her siblings had spent hours desperately seeking answers after the pilot of their parents' plane had issued a Mayday call only to then go radio silent.

Never to be heard from again.

Oh yeah. It was only a matter of time before the Sullivan siblings would converge on this area to begin another search.

He didn't want any of them to be in danger, especially not Jessica. He reminded himself that Maya was a former cop married to Doug who happened to be a current criminal investigator. They should be able to keep the younger siblings from making any hasty decisions.

Or so he hoped.

Logan alternated between scanning their surroundings and watching Jess's K9, Teddy. He knew the dog would pick up on any unusual scents or threats before he would.

When Jess slipped again, he lengthened his stride to catch up to her. "Time for another break."

"But we're so close," she protested. "Isn't that the clearing up ahead?"

"Yes. This distance can be deceiving, though." He nudged her toward a fallen tree. "Just sit down for a few minutes, okay? We'll be on our way out of here soon."

She sighed and nodded. Despite her desire to push forward, she looked exhausted. They'd come down the mountainside at a quick pace. He turned to stare behind them. There was a slim chance the shooter had kept pace, looking for an opportunity to take another shot.

If the intent was to kill them, he figured the shooter would have kept firing at them. His gut told him that the shots had been a warning for them to get out of the area.

There was no sign of anyone behind them. Yet those footprints heading away from the location where they'd been targeted bothered him. He should have paid closer attention on their way up to retrieve the chunk of metal.

If he'd have noticed the tracks, he'd have been on alert for danger. Maybe even going back to the plane for his weapon.

Thankfully, Jess and Teddy hadn't been hurt. Or

worse. But he grimly knew the outcome could have been much different.

Teddy lifted his snout to sniff the air. When the dog didn't sense anything amiss, he tried to relax. His Cessna was only a couple hundred yards away. They'd be packed up and in the air within the hour.

"We should have dropped a few neon markers back there," Jess said with a sigh. "I'm such an idiot. Without marking the location, I'm concerned we won't find the exact spot when we return with law enforcement."

Doing that hadn't occurred to him. He wasn't aware that she even had markers. They must have been a search and rescue thing. "I have the compass coordinates. We'll get close enough using them."

She frowned. "We? There's no reason to drag you back here."

"Oh yeah there is." He glanced around the area again before meeting her gaze. "If you're coming back, so am I. Besides, I'm convinced the shooting is related to that guy who chartered a flight from Cheyenne. If so, I want to be sure we find him."

After a few minutes of silence, she nodded and rose to her feet. "Fine. I guess I can't stop you. But for now, let's get to the plane. I'm anxious to talk this through with Doug and Maya as soon as possible."

"Okay." He gestured for her to take the lead. "I'm right behind you."

Fifteen minutes later, they reached the edge of the clearing. In the center of the makeshift runway, his Cessna sat waiting for them. From what he could tell, it hadn't been tampered with. He'd know more when they got closer.

Jess stopped and glanced back at him. "We'll be out in the open from this point forward."

"I know." He didn't like the lack of cover either. "I'll stay behind you. Try to keep Teddy out in front."

"Okay." She shot him a worried glance, then gestured toward her dog. "Are you ready? Let's go, Teddy."

Teddy moved out first. Jess quickly ran out from the woods to keep up with her dog. Logan followed suit, putting on a burst of speed despite the heavy weight of the pack.

They reached the plane without incident. He drew her around to the passenger side, then wrenched the door open. "You and Teddy jump in." He helped her out of the backpack, then shrugged his off too. He stored them both inside, then stepped back. "I need to check the bird before we take off."

"Okay. Up, Teddy." Jess gestured with her hand. The dog looked at her, then gathered himself to make the leap. "Good boy," she praised, before climbing in.

Logan felt better knowing Jess and Teddy were

inside the plane. Not that it was bulletproof, but at least they weren't out in the open. He quickly checked the surface of his craft, making sure no one had tampered with it in any way. He even bent to examine the wheels, relieved to note they looked good.

When that was done, he opened the door of the cockpit and climbed inside. He started the engine, listening for a long moment. Satisfied it sounded normal, he closed the door, double-checked his fuel gauge, then pulled his headphones on. Plane engines were too loud for anyone to fly without them. It always made him smile that Jess put a set of earmuffs over Teddy's ears.

"Are you okay?" He glanced at Jess.

"Yes." She made a thumbs-up gesture. "I'll be glad to get out of here."

No lie, he thought as he turned the plane around. The more he thought about the gunfire incident, the more convinced he was that the shooter was warning them off. Maybe they'd gotten too close to whatever illegal drug trade Benton had going on.

Every time he heard about drugs, he thought of Ella. Of how she'd died of a drug overdose the night after they'd argued.

The night he'd broken up with Ella, secretly acknowledging the feelings he'd had for Jess.

He shook off the troubling thoughts. He needed to concentrate on getting the Cessna airborne. He increased his speed, the propellers whirling loudly beneath the wings. Then he pulled back on the yoke, taking them upward. Off the ground and into the air.

This was the part he loved the most about flying. Floating in the air, high above the earth below. He continued climbing upward.

Then the plane jolted beneath his fingers.

What in the world? He continued pulling the yoke, but the plane listed to one side. And that's when he realized they'd been hit.

"What's wrong?" Jessica asked fearfully. "Is there a problem with the engine?"

Yeah, there was a problem all right. He felt certain the shooter had tracked alongside them all the way back to the plane, waiting until they were airborne to take one last shot at them.

So much for simply warning them off. This guy was obviously playing for keeps.

"Mayday, Mayday." He toggled the switch for the radio as he fought to keep the plane level. "This is flight 257, repeat, flight 257. We've been hit and will need to make an emergency landing."

There was nothing but silence. The radio transmission had not gone through. Likely because they weren't high enough in altitude.

There wasn't time to keep trying. He banked the plane into a curve, knowing he had little choice but to head back to land on the makeshift airstrip they'd just left to attempt an emergency landing.

The one where the shooter could very well be waiting.

The plane continued to list to one side, making it difficult to keep its wings level. That wasn't a good sign for landing. If the wing struck the ground, the entire plane could flip over.

He gently eased back on his speed, hoping to glide along with the wind as he approached the landing strip. He glanced at Jess who had reached back to hold on to Teddy's vest and began to pray.

"Lord Jesus, keep us safe in Your care! Guide us to safety!" Her voice became choked. "Let thy will be done. Amen!"

"Amen," he echoed. Then he added, "Hang on. It's going to be a rough landing." He lowered the plane closer to the ground, sweat beading on his forehead as he struggled to keep the plane level. The wheels beneath the belly of the plane touched the ground briefly, then the bird bounced up again.

Gritting his teeth, he tried again. They needed to get on the ground in one piece. "Gently, gently," he whispered.

This time, the wheels touched the ground and stayed there. He slowed their speed even further as they rolled across the open field. He didn't relax his grip on the yoke until he'd brought the plane to a shuddering stop.

"Thank You, God!" Jessica said. "You did it, Logan! We made it!"

"Yeah." He frowned, then started the engine again. He'd aimed for the center of the airstrip but decided that wasn't their best option. "We made it this far. Let's see if we can get a little farther."

"What are you talking about?" Jess sounded panicked. "We're not going back up into the air, are we?"

"No, we won't leave the ground." He turned the plane toward the opposite side of the woods from where they'd headed off earlier that day. Within minutes, they were rolling across the airstrip and crashing into the woods. He pushed the plane as far as he dared, branches slapping against the wings and the windows until the brush was so thick they couldn't go any farther. "This is it," he said, bringing the bird to a grinding halt.

"Why did you crash us into the woods?" Jess asked.

"Because we need cover to get out of here." He pushed open his door. "We don't know where the gunman is located."

"Gunman?" The color leeched from her face. "That's what happened? He shot at us?"

"Oh yeah." He jumped down and then opened the door to the back seat for the backpack. He removed the tail piece, as they couldn't lug it across the wilderness. Then he reached for his personal survival pack. He kept one stored on the plane just for this reason. It had been two years since he'd last had to use it, but he was grateful for the backup supplies now. The tent and sleeping bag might come in handy.

He bent forward to grab the radio out of the Cessna. Maybe once they were in another location, he could get it to work long enough to call for help.

Lastly, he opened the box containing his handgun. He tucked the weapon into his coat pocket along with the extra cartridge of shells. He needed to be prepared for any threat, either from the gunman or other wild animals.

On the other side of the plane, Jess had gotten Teddy down onto the ground and was reassuring the dog that they would be okay. He hoped and prayed she was right.

They had to move, to get as far away from the plane as possible.

From this point forward, they were on their own.

3

———

"We're going to be okay," Jess told Teddy as she pulled the duffel full of dog supplies from the plane and hefted it over her shoulder. "Once we're safe, we'll call for help."

Teddy's ears were pricked forward, his dark eyes steady on hers. She knew the dog probably didn't understand what she was saying, but she hoped her soothing tone was reassuring.

She needed that—more so than he did.

"Jess?" Logan's low voice wafted toward her. "We need to move."

She hiked up the duffel, realizing it was too big to lug through the woods. She carried it around the nose of the plane to where Logan was rearranging items in the backpack. "Wait. I have supplies for Teddy that we need to take with us."

He paused, then nodded. "Okay. How much room do you need?"

She dropped the duffel, then knelt beside him. "How long do you think we'll be gone? I'd like to take at least enough dog food for twenty-four to forty-eight hours." That was probably overkill, but she would not shortchange her K9.

"Sounds good. Hopefully, we won't be gone that long."

She pulled out the gallon-sized plastic bag of dog food and stuffed it into the backpack, then added several water bottles. Lastly, she took the booties from the duffel and placed them over Teddy's paws. The dog didn't love wearing them, but he didn't try to take them off either, the way Chase's K9 did.

Once they set off through the terrain, Teddy would forget he was wearing them.

"This is going to be heavy for you," Logan warned as he lifted the backpack. "Mine is bigger, so you'll need to take this one."

"I can manage." She slid one arm through the strap, stifling a groan as she bent forward to get her other arm through. He was right. It was heavy.

"Let's go." Logan took a moment to toss the now half-empty duffel back into the plane, along with the section of tail they'd come all this way to retrieve. She hated leaving it behind but understood they couldn't carry it along with their supplies. They needed to prepare for the likely scenario that they might be out there all night.

She planned to call her family for help, but it would take her siblings time to get there. Especially if they needed to charter a plane from someone other than Logan. And even then, she worried that bringing them to this location would place them in the crosshairs of danger.

It would be better for her and Logan to hike to a new location. Maybe someplace where her family could drive instead of fly?

What was the gunman up to anyway? Why try to take them down?

"Take the lead," Logan said, keeping his voice low. "I'll cover your back."

She swallowed hard. "Okay, but I'm not sure where we're headed."

"Just go southwest for now." He shrugged. "But we're going to stay in the woods as much as possible."

"Southwest through the woods. Got it." She drew in a steadying breath, then gave Teddy the hand signal to come. Thankfully, her K9 was a high-energy dog. He gracefully leaped over some low brush to reach her side.

They didn't talk as they walked. Logan didn't tell her to hurry, but she sensed his urgency to put distance between them and the shooter.

She wanted that, too, so she walked as fast as she could while carrying the heavy pack. Every so often, she pulled her cell phone out to check for a signal.

No bars. With a sense of trepidation, she stopped checking. There was no point in asking Logan if he had service. If she didn't have any, he wouldn't either. There weren't cell towers in the mountains.

Was that the reason the shooter had chosen this location for whatever illegal business he was involved in? She had to assume those illegal activities were the reason he'd taken shots at them.

Not just shots, she silently amended. This guy had attempted to kill them by shooting down their plane.

She shivered at their near miss. If not for Logan's expertise in landing the damaged plane, they'd have died.

Just like her parents had.

She and Logan hiked for thirty minutes straight before she stopped near a thick oak tree. Teddy took advantage of the moment by dropping down beside her. She shrugged out of the overstuffed backpack to give her K9 some water. Logan joined her. "I haven't heard anyone following so far."

She nodded. "I guess that's good. Do you think anyone heard your call for help via the radio? Before we made that crash landing?"

"Doubtful." He scanned their surroundings. "I brought the radio with me. We'll try again later. For now, it's more important to get away from the gunman."

"True." She sighed. "I was just hoping . . ."

"I know your family will worry," he finished for her. "Hopefully, we'll get through on the radio to reassure them that we're not hurt."

"It's fine." She forced a smile. "They'll have faith in God, in our ability to be prepared enough to survive this."

He nodded. "At some point, we'll get into cell tower range."

"That would help." She stroked a hand over Teddy's fur, then glanced up at the clouds darkening the sky. Was snow in the forecast? It wouldn't be the first time it snowed in April. "I hope we're not stuck out here all night."

"I have a small tent and camping gear," Logan said. "We'll be okay." But his gaze was full of concern too. "The main thing is to make sure we're far away from the shooter before we even consider bunking down for the night."

She tried not to imagine sharing a tent with Logan and Teddy. Being in an enclosed space would be vastly different from simply hiking side by side. But this wasn't the time to think about that. She glanced at her watch. "It's going on four o'clock in the afternoon."

"I know." He rose to his feet and grabbed his extra-large backpack. She imagined his was far heavier than hers if there was a tent and other camping gear inside. She forced herself upright too. Logan helped her with the backpack, settling it on her shoulders.

"Thanks." She did her best not to show her fatigue. She'd been on numerous search and rescue missions that often lasted for days, but she felt oddly exhausted now as they continued on their southwestern path heading away from the wrecked plane.

Maybe because there was no end in sight.

She pushed that thought away, keeping a wary eye on Teddy as they continued foraging through the woods. Not following a path made it harder to make good time. She understood the need to put distance between them and the bad guy, but she wouldn't risk her K9.

Even if that meant carrying him.

No easy task as Teddy was eighty pounds of solid muscle. She told herself not to worry as they continued cutting a trail through the woods. They could do this.

Failure wasn't an option.

Another thirty minutes later, Teddy started looking up at her as if silently asking how much longer? She grimaced and glanced back at Logan. His grim expression indicated he didn't think they'd gone far enough.

"Soon, Teddy," she promised. Looking ahead, she searched for a logical place to stop for a while. Despite their lunch sandwich, her stomach was growling with hunger, and she'd have to feed Teddy dinner as well.

The sound of trickling water caught her attention. She quickened her pace, hoping there was a stream nearby. Teddy, of course, found it before she did. He rushed ahead, and she heard him slurping water. Knowing the water source was likely snow melting off the mountains, she wasn't too concerned.

A moment later, she found the stream. Teddy was lying on his stomach near the bank as if he had no intention of moving anytime soon.

"This must be part of Shell Creek," Logan said as he joined her. "You can see the peak of Snowshoe Mountain."

One mountain looked much like the other to her, but she trusted Logan's judgment. "Teddy needs a break." She sighed and dropped the pack from her aching shoulders. "To be honest, I do too."

"I hear you." He shrugged out of his pack as well. "We can stay here for a while. But I don't think we should set up our camp just yet."

Her spirits plummeted. "We've been hiking for over an hour."

"I know, but we've only covered about two miles, maybe a little more." He grimaced. "We'll see. I just don't want the gunman to show up while we're asleep."

The very thought of that made her grimace. "That would not be good. We can keep going if you think that's best."

"I do." He held her gaze. "I'm sorry, Jess. I feel bad I've dragged you and Teddy into the middle of this."

"Not your fault. I wanted to find that piece of plane very badly." She sighed. "Truthfully, I'm the one who drew you into this. And we don't even know that the tail fin is related to my parents' crash." She tried not to sound as depressed as she felt. "We could be going through all this for nothing."

"Hey, we're going to be fine." He sat beside her and wrapped his arm around her shoulders. "I'll protect you and so will Teddy. As far as the plane piece, it's so rusted I'm sure it's been out here for years. Once we're back home, we'll have it tested.

This was something we needed to do, Jess. I'm here for you."

"You're sweet, Logan." She rested her head against his shoulder. "I know we're going to be fine. At least it's not January."

"For sure," he agreed.

They sat in silence for a long moment. Thanks to the clouds darkening the sky, the temperature was dropping like a rock. She understood they would need to keep moving to take advantage of what was left of the natural light.

Hiking in darkness was a surefire way to get hurt. Not just for her and Logan, but Teddy too.

"Let's keep pushing forward for another half hour," she suggested. "We'll need to stop long enough to feed Teddy."

"Okay." He waved a hand toward the stream. "I think we should be okay to follow this down for a while."

"That would be great." Walking along the creek bank would be easier than cutting through thick brush. "My main concern is Teddy. He'll push himself to the brink of exhaustion for me if I let him."

"We won't allow that happen." He glanced up at the sky. "Although we'll need to pray the snow holds off a bit. At least until we can make camp."

She shivered, even though she wasn't cold. Their

hike had kept her warm, but that could soon change.

They didn't need fresh snow on top of being stranded on the side of the mountain. She lifted her eyes to the sky and prayed for God to guide them to safety.

LOGAN BATTLED guilt as they continued their trek down the mountain. He hoped that following the creek would make things easier. He had noticed Teddy seeming to lag behind a bit and knew they wouldn't be able to push on for much longer. He wished they could get farther away from the plane, but he took some comfort in the fact that the gunman wouldn't want to hike through the woods at night any more than they did.

And maybe the gunman didn't have camping gear either. When he'd dropped Craig Benton, or whatever his name was, off here in the Bighorns, he'd assumed the guy was meeting up with his buddies at a hunting cabin. He hadn't seen one, but figured there must be one close by. If that was true, the guy wouldn't want to get too far away from his home base.

Unless he was that determined to kill them.

Logan knew better than to dwell on what-if scenarios. As a pilot, he knew how to create an alternate plan—one made by facing the facts as they were presented.

The good news was that he hadn't heard anyone moving through the woods as if following them. Either the gunman had given up the chase or he was far enough back that he couldn't be heard.

He was hoping for the former.

"Logan, is that a cabin up ahead?" Jess gestured toward the east. "Maybe there's a fireplace or wood-burning stove."

He quickly identified the structure she was talking about. "Yeah, I think that's an old hunting shanty. The DNR put several of them up decades ago. None had woodstoves as far as I know. The few I've seen up close were falling apart."

"Oh, okay." She looked depressed. "I was hoping we could use it."

He hated disappointing her. As they continued to walk, he considered their options. If the gunman was on their trail, the shanty would be an obvious spot to search for them. Then again, if the gunman had given up trying to track them down, the shanty would offer some shelter from the snow he felt certain loomed on the horizon.

Finally, he relented. "Okay, let's head over to check it out. If the roof isn't collapsing in on itself, we can consider staying inside. Or we can set up the tent nearby using the structure to block the wind."

"That would be great." She gestured toward Teddy. "I can tell he's getting tired."

"We all are," he agreed. "We'll need to find a place to cross the stream."

After another seventy yards, Jess stopped. "This should work. See that flat rock? We can use it as a steppingstone."

"Okay, but it's going to be slippery. We need to find a stick too." He turned to scan their surroundings.

Jess picked up one stick, then another. "They're too short," she said with a frown.

He walked a little farther and found a stick that was almost five feet long. He quickly carried it back to her. "Here, use this. You go first." He glanced at the dog. "Teddy might have to get wet."

"He should be okay, if we can start a fire so he can dry off." She took the stick from his grasp. "I'll cross first with Teddy. Then I'll toss the stick back over to you."

"Sounds good." He would have offered to carry the dog, but with his pack and the slick rock, he didn't think that would work. "We'll definitely start a fire."

"Okay, let's do this." She turned toward the narrow spot of the creek. "Come, Teddy."

Logan found himself holding his breath as she extended her leg to reach the slick rock. Using the stick as a lever, she managed to shift her weight from the foot on the bank to the one on the rock. With the grace of a dancer, she then pivoted to reach the other side. Teddy splashed through the creek without concern. Then he quickly shook himself off.

"Stand back. Stick is coming your way." Jess threw it like a javelin. He let it hit the ground, then reached for it.

He quickly joined her on the other side. He kept the stick, knowing it would be helpful in building the fire.

Twenty minutes later, they reached the shanty. He followed Jessica inside, only to hear her groan.

"Half the roof is gone!" She gestured up at the gaping hole over their heads.

"I told you it would be in rough shape." He glanced around the interior where many forest animals had clearly made themselves at home. "The wind is coming in from the west. We'll set up the tent on the east side of the building. That, along with the fire, should help keep us warm."

"Okay." She managed a smile. "I'm sure we'll be fine. Especially now that we can rest for a while."

He nodded, knowing he wouldn't be able to rest until he'd set up their camp and had a fire going.

Turning, he went outside to the east side of the shanty. There was an open area that appeared relatively flat. He shrugged off his backpack and went to work setting up the small pup tent. He had a small thermal pad to line the bottom, which would help keep them insulated.

To his surprise, Jess didn't sit down to rest. She dropped her backpack, rolled her shoulders to work the kinks out, then began gathering wood for their fire. He couldn't help but smile as he put the tent up. Being stuck on the mountain with Jessica was no hardship. In other circumstances, this could be a date.

But not when they were only there because a gunman had attempted to shoot down his plane.

"I don't suppose you have a lighter," she asked.

"I do." He rummaged in the pack that was half empty now that he had the tent up and the sleeping bag unzipped and spread out inside. He tossed the lighter to her, and she lit the small branches she'd gathered, blowing gently to get the flames to catch.

"Who taught you to camp?" he asked, once she had the fire going well enough to add larger branches. "Chase?"

"Yep." She drew Teddy closer to the fire. The dog stretched out beside her, resting his head on her knee. Then the K9 let out a heavy sigh and closed his eyes. She stroked his fur. "He made sure we all know how to set up a makeshift camp in the woods. I was probably sixteen back then, and he'd just opened his hunting and fishing guide business." She nodded toward the fire. "He insisted we learn how to start a blaze without a lighter, using flint stone, but it's much easier this way."

He chuckled. "That's true. We can eat our protein bars and some of the dried fruit and nut snacks for dinner. We may want to save the rest for morning."

"Sounds good to me." She frowned and rummaged in her backpack for Teddy's food. "Actually, I have four granola bars too." She grinned. "If I had remembered having them, I probably would have eaten them by now. But this way we have breakfast and lunch. Not too shabby."

"We won't starve." He hoped they'd be able to head out at first light. He pulled the radio out of his pack and tried to get a signal. There was nothing but static. He shoved the radio aside and checked his cell phone. No service there either. With a sigh, he gave up. If they ended up staying a second night, he'd have to hunt for small game or maybe try catching some fish. He wasn't the expert Chase was, but he'd done his fair share of hunting and fishing.

He watched as Jess filled a collapsible bowl with food for Teddy. Despite his obvious fatigue, the K9 eagerly jumped up to eat. Logan dropped down beside Jess with the rations of food. They ate in silence, watching the crackling fire and basking in the warmth from the flames. Using what was left of the hunting shanty as a wind block helped keep the temperature up.

But the clouds overhead had grown dark and thick with moisture. Once it started snowing, they'd lose the fire and would be forced to rely on body heat to stay warm inside the tent.

When they finished eating, he reached for his backpack. "We need to store our stuff inside the tent to keep the animals away. And we'll use our outer coats as an extra layer of insulation. Between the thermal pad on the bottom of the tent and the sleeping bag that I've opened to use as a blanket, we should be okay."

"I'm sure we will." She managed to sound confident.

He shoved his pack through the opening, then turned to face her. "I need to check the perimeter. Ah, you may need to find some privacy among the bushes too." He hoped she couldn't see his face turning red with embarrassment. "I'll stay away long enough for you to finish up." He cleared his throat, feeling awkward. "Once you and Teddy crawl into the tent, I'll know the coast is clear."

"That works. Teddy will need to relieve himself too." She leaned forward to run her bare fingers over his lower legs. "Wow, I'm impressed. His fur is already dry."

"Good." He knew her first concern would always be her dog. He quickly rose to his feet and headed away from their camp. When he rounded the corner of the shanty, the wind hit him full in the face.

It was going to be a cold night. Hopefully cold enough to keep the gunman back in his warm hunting cabin.

After taking care of his needs, Logan walked the perimeter, scanning the area for signs of an intruder. He also wanted to make sure Jess had more than enough time to get settled in. Thankfully, he didn't see anything suspicious. He completed his loop around the shanty, nodding with satisfaction when he returned to the camp to see a faint glow coming from inside the tent. He could see the shadows of Jessica and Teddy as she moved what must have been a flashlight from side to side.

The fire was slowly burning out, so he waited a few minutes, then kicked the glowing coals apart to hasten the process. Just as the fire was out and no longer a threat, the snow began to fall, fat snowflakes hitting his face and melting instantly against his skin.

Just in time, he thought, as he dropped to his knees beside the tent opening. "Coming in," he announced as he unzipped the flap.

"It's going to be a tight fit," Jess said as he crawled in. She was using her backpack as a pillow. "I don't think this tent was made for two people and a large dog."

She was right about that. He wiggled out of his winter coat, setting it around his side of the tent. "Better than sleeping outside in the snow."

"Snow? Really?" Her eyes widened in surprise. "I had hoped it would hold off."

"Unfortunately, it's coming down." He wiggled around so he could close the zipper. He made sure the two window flaps were open just enough to provide some ventilation, then he lifted one edge of the sleeping bag to slide beneath. "Do you want Teddy between us?"

"Ah, he's probably better at my side." She sounded slightly nervous. "He moves around a lot at night."

"You're safe with me, Jess." He stretched out beneath the sleeping bag and adjusted his pack as a pillow as well.

"I know that." She wiggled closer, rearranged the blanket to help cover Teddy too. Then doused the flashlight. "I trust you, Logan."

"Thanks." He should have been exhausted after their long day, but the enticing scent of her hair teased his senses. He did his best to ignore the sweetness. It wasn't just that Jess trusted him. He knew the entire Sullivan family expected him to treat Jessica with respect and to do everything possible to keep her safe.

And he would. No matter what.

When Teddy began to snore, he couldn't help but laugh. Jess did too. "He's funny, isn't he?" she whispered.

"Yep." She turned on her side so that she was facing him. Then she yawned. "G'night, Logan."

"Good night." He closed his eyes and told himself to go to sleep.

Of course, that didn't work. He listened to the sounds of the night outside their tent, and to Jess's soft breathing and Teddy's snores. He thought about how much damage his plane had sustained and hoped it wouldn't take them too long to get to a location with radio or cell service.

He must have dozed at some point because he awoke when Teddy began to bark. Not just once, but repeated sharp barks that were clearly a response to a perceived threat.

Logan jackknifed upright and grabbed his .38 from the backpack, his heart pounding in his chest.

Someone was out there!

4

―――――――

Disoriented by Teddy's sharp barking, Jess sat up, pushing her hair from her eyes. It took a second for her to realize she was camping outside in the mountains with Logan rather than being at home on the Sullivan ranch.

"Easy, boy." She tried to soothe her K9. But Teddy wasn't having it. He continued to bark at some unknown threat.

Her blood ran cold when she saw the weapon Logan had set on the ground beside him. He was dragging his outer gear on with jerky movements, no easy task in the small confines of the tent. His expression grim, Logan whispered, "Stay here with Teddy. I'll check it out."

She was torn between keeping her dog safe and

letting Teddy head out to help find the intruder. Yet she couldn't sit there and wait for him to face the threat alone.

She reached for her coat. "Better that we stick together."

Logan frowned but didn't argue. He finished lacing his boots, then unzipped the front flap. It was only when he poked his head out, bringing in a rush of cold air, that she realized how warm and snug the tent had been. More so than she'd expected.

Over Logan's shoulder, she could only see the blinding whiteness of freshly fallen snow blanketing the ground as early morning light dawned on the horizon. Maybe the few inches of snow on their tent had added a layer of insulation. "Wait for me," she said, shoving her feet into her boots.

"I don't see any footprints in the snow outside our tent." Logan's voice was low and husky. "Teddy's barking may have scared him off."

Scared whom off? The gunman? She swallowed hard and took a moment to fasten Teddy's vest and to slide the booties over his feet. He was too busy barking to protest the booties. Her K9's body vibrated with his need to rush outside to face the threat. She didn't like this scenario one bit, but they had little choice but to act. Drawing a steadying breath, she whispered, "Okay. We're ready."

"Stay behind me as much as possible." Logan

crawled from the tent and quickly rose to his feet, holding the weapon ready as he walked forward. She went through the flap first, then held it for Teddy.

Her K9 bounded out and ran full steam ahead through the snow. Seconds later, Teddy rounded the corner of the hunting shanty.

So much for staying behind Logan.

"Teddy, heel!" Her command seemed to evaporate on the wind. Teddy was normally well trained, but this time he ignored her command. Logan clumsily ran through the newly fallen snow, following Teddy's lead. She did her best to keep up.

It didn't take long to find the tracks. Not animal, as she'd hoped. No, these were definitely human footprints in the snow. Teddy sniffed the ground and started to follow them up the slope of the hill.

"Teddy, come!" She spoke in a harsh tone, and this time, her K9 responded. He took another long second to sniff the footprints, then wheeled around to trot back to her side. His tail wagged from side to side as if pleased with his job of scaring off danger.

"I'm amazed Teddy heard this guy way over here." Logan gestured to the hill behind the hunting shanty as he scanned their surroundings. "Looks to me like he started coming down toward the shanty, then turned around when Teddy started barking. It took us a while to get outside the tent to find him.

By now, he's probably headed back to wherever he came from."

"Unless he's looping around to try again?" She made a 360-degree turn, scanning their surroundings the way Logan had. Jess wished she'd thought to bring her weapon along. It hadn't seemed necessary for a quick plane ride to retrieve a piece from a plane.

Never again would she be caught off guard. Like Logan, she needed to be prepared for anything.

"I don't understand why he took off." She glanced back at Logan. "The gunman knew we had Teddy with us, so he should have anticipated the dog would bark. And we were all together in one spot. Why not just start firing at us through the tent? He could have taken us all out of the picture without a problem."

"I'm not sure." Logan scowled. "Could be he didn't see the tent, as it was covered in snow. Or maybe someone other than the gunman was out taking a walk."

"In this weather?" She scoffed. "Doubtful."

"I don't know, and it doesn't really matter. Thanks to Teddy, we're fine." He shoved his weapon into his pocket. "Time for us to get out of here."

She nodded, more than happy to go along with that plan. They turned to head back to their tent. Breaking down their camp took longer than she liked, and Jess found herself glancing over her shoulder frequently to make sure nobody was out there.

They had Teddy as a watchdog, but remembering how the gunman had fired upon them with a rifle made her think the intruder could have retreated far enough to set up someplace, waiting for them to head out again.

"I wish we could follow those footprints." She glanced at Logan as she filled Teddy's bowl with food. "I keep thinking he's positioned somewhere nearby where he might try to take another shot at us."

"I'm concerned about the possibility too," Logan agreed. "I don't like knowing we're vulnerable out here."

Vulnerable was putting it mildly. Shoving items into her backpack, which was slightly lighter this morning after feeding Teddy twice since they'd started this adventure, she watched as Logan made quick work of packing his tent and sleeping bag in the larger pack. He worked quickly and efficiently. Then he stood and helped her with her backpack. When Teddy finished eating, Logan added the collapsible bowl to her gear.

She'd almost suggested leaving the tent behind but knew that would be foolish. If something happened and they didn't get off this mountain, they'd need shelter. Food, too, but shelter was more important than anything else.

And while she knew her family was likely hitting the road this morning to find them, she wasn't sure how successful their efforts would be. If Logan's Mayday call hadn't gone through, her siblings would only have a vague flight plan to work from.

That hadn't worked so well in finding her parents' plane. Over five years later and they still hadn't recovered their plane or their remains. She knew only too well the same thing could happen again here.

"We'll eat our protein bars later," Logan said, breaking into her thoughts. "We need to get as far away from this location as possible."

"Okay." She knew he wanted her to head out first, so she strode forward. Teddy stayed close to her side. "We're still heading southwest?"

"Yeah," Logan agreed. "For now."

If she'd thought hiking yesterday was difficult, today was worse. They didn't have snowshoes, which would have made it easier. There was only about four inches of snow covering the ground, so she knew it could be worse.

But the snow covered the potential hazards of rocks and fallen logs. She also kept glancing over her shoulder, fearing they'd be targeted by gunfire at any minute.

Thankfully, nobody shot at them. And after they'd walked for a full hour, Logan called out, "Break time."

"Thank you, Lord," she whispered. She stopped and turned to wait for Logan to catch up to her. "We should be safe by now."

"I think so." He took off his pack and rummaged inside. "Here." He handed her a protein bar. "Let's eat now."

Her stomach was rumbling, and the protein bar didn't do much to take the edge off her hunger. She didn't complain, though. They were alive and unharmed.

Based on the footprints located near their camp, she knew the outcome could have been much worse.

"Maybe we should try the radio." She tucked the wrapper of her protein bar in her pocket. "Or our phones. Looks like the sky is clearing up, maybe we'll get a signal soon."

Logan glanced around. "Let's go a little farther before we take the time to do that. I want to be sure we're safe."

Teddy stood, his nose to the air sniffing intently. Since his initial barking frenzy, he'd been calm and quiet. She rested her hand on Teddy's head. "I'm trusting you to alert us to danger, okay, big guy?"

Teddy gazed at her with his dark-brown eyes as if in agreement.

She turned and continued walking, staying within the shelter of the trees as much as possible. The going was slower than she liked, but every step was progress.

They walked in silence, partially because she needed her strength to keep moving and also to avoid drawing attention to themselves. Their movements weren't completely silent, though. Twigs snapped and snow crunched beneath their feet.

After another forty-five minutes of walking, Logan called for another break. She gratefully dropped onto the horizontal surface of a fallen tree. "This is quite the workout," she muttered.

"I know." Logan sat beside her and pulled his phone from his pack. He held it up and peered at the screen. "No service."

She wasn't surprised. "What about the radio?"

He shoved the phone into the pack, then drew out the small radio. After fiddling with the controls for a few minutes and hearing nothing but static, he finally found a channel. "Mayday, this is pilot Logan Fletcher. Anyone read me?"

"I read you, Fletcher, where are you?" a voice asked.

"We're northeast of Snowshoe Mountain." Logan grinned, and she found herself grinning back. "We're on foot but will need someone to meet us if possible."

"Roger that, Fletcher. Chase Sullivan and his brother Shane are on the road heading to the Bigho"—the radio dispatcher's voice broke up with static but then came through again—"them know your coordinates."

As Logan recited their latitude and longitude coordinates, Jess rested her hand on Teddy's neck and lifted her gaze to the sky in gratitude.

Help was on the way.

"CAN you get to the Cabin Creek Campsite?" the radio dispatcher asked a few minutes later.

"Yes, we can get there," Logan assured him.

"Chase and Shane will rendezvous with you there."

"Roger that." Logan was relieved to know the Sullivans were en route to pick them up, but they still had a long way to go. The Cabin Creek Campsite was at least five miles away. Maybe longer. Five miles over rough terrain would take them a solid three hours.

The good news was that he was convinced the gunman was no longer a threat. He still wasn't sure who had approached their camp in the first place.

As Jess had pointed out, the gunman could have emptied his clip on the tent, killing them in one fell swoop. Logan had to believe the tent hadn't been readily visible beneath the snow.

Could the intruder have mistaken Teddy's barking for that of a coyote? That didn't seem logical. But then again, none of this made any sense. He couldn't fathom why anyone would have tried to shoot his plane out of the sky in the first place.

"How far is the campsite?" Jess asked as he packed the radio away. She was stroking Teddy's soft fur, either to keep her dog calm or for her own peace of mind. "I've never stayed there."

"Roughly five miles." He forced a reassuring smile. "Piece of cake after everything we've been through."

"Right." She stopped petting Teddy to rummage in her backpack. She pulled out two granola bars. "This is all I have left, but since we only have another five miles to go, there's no sense in holding on to them."

He nodded and accepted the nourishment. They'd been burning a lot of calories since heading out that morning. He quickly ate the bar, then pulled out his compass to verify their coordinates.

"Let's head due west for a bit," he suggested.

"You're the boss." Jess finished her granola bar

and shouldered her pack. "It's nice to have a firm destination in mind."

He realized he should have mentioned his plan earlier. He'd been too busy glancing back over his shoulder to make sure they weren't being followed.

"The Cabin Creek Campsite isn't that far from Highway 14," he explained as they continued forging a path through the woods. "There's a smaller road that heads from the highway to the campground. Cabin Creek is a popular spot in the summer. Not so much this time of the year."

"I'll just be glad to be safe." She sighed. "It's really bothering me that someone tried to kill us by shooting at your plane."

"Yeah, me too." He lifted his arm to prevent a low-hanging branch from slapping him in the face. "I keep going back to that guy I dropped off."

"Craig Benton," she said with a scowl. "Or whatever his real name is."

"Yep, him. I think he's involved in moving drugs, and it was either him or one of his accomplices who shot at us." He grimaced, watching as Teddy nimbly leaped over a fallen branch. Not only had Teddy alerted on the scent of drugs on Benton's glove, but the K9 had also saved their lives by alerting them to danger this morning.

"I don't remember seeing a cabin, do you?" Jess asked.

"Nope. And I remember looking around for a dwelling of some sort after I dropped him off."

"Maybe it was hidden behind a part of the mountain." Jess tripped over a rock but caught herself. "Or it was camouflaged in some way."

"Could be." If the dwelling was some sort of hideout for drug runners, he was sure that it would have been built in a way to blend into the surroundings.

"We'll find it," Jess said confidently.

He sighed. They weren't even off the mountain yet, and she was already planning her next trip back to search for the gunman, using Teddy to find any narcotics in the area. Logan made a mental note to pull Chase aside to make sure her older brother understood the risk. Teddy might be a trained narcotics dog, but law enforcement officials needed to take the lead on this search.

Not the Sullivan family.

They walked for the next hour in silence, the sun warming the air enough that the snow began to melt. Jessica stopped mostly in deference to her dog.

"He's getting tired," she said, when they sat down to rest. As if to prove her point, Teddy stretched out on the ground beside her and closed his eyes.

He was jealous of the K9's ability to fall asleep on a dime.

"We're making good time." He checked his compass again. "We have a little less than three miles to go."

"Three miles." She let out a low groan. "I hope Teddy can hold up for that long."

He rested against a tree trunk. "He seems to be doing pretty well. I haven't noticed his energy lagging the way it did last night."

"Not yet, but we've covered a lot of ground already this morning. Hopefully, these breaks will help hold him over until we can reach the campground." She sighed and stifled a yawn. "I'd give a lot for a large cup of coffee."

"Ditto." He tried not to think about how hungry he was. The protein and granola bars hadn't been as satisfying as he'd hoped. Better than nothing, of course. Still, he found himself dreaming about coffee and breakfast.

The sound of a phone ringing startled them both. Teddy barely opened one eye, then closed it again.

"We have cell service!" Jess pulled her phone from her pack and showed him the screen. "My brother."

"Put it on speaker," he suggested.

"Hi, Chase. You're on speaker," Jessica said. "Can you hear me?"

"Where have you been?" Chase sounded upset.

"What's with you taking off with Logan without saying anything?"

Logan hid a wince. *Way to get on Chase's bad side.*

"My fault, it was supposed to be a quick flight," Jess said. "Logan spotted a section of plane on the mountain. We went to grab it and ran into some trouble."

"Don't tell me Logan crashed his plane," Chase sounded incredulous.

"Only after someone took a shot at us as we were taking off," Logan interjected. "I'm sorry about all of this. It wasn't my intent to put Jessica in danger."

"Shot at you?" Chase echoed.

"It's a long story." Jess pinned him with a dark look. Clearly, she hadn't wanted Logan to mention the gunfire. "We'll fill you in when we meet up with you at the campground. Logan says we're shy of three miles away."

"That's fine. We're hoping to be there in about an hour," Chase said. "The highway is drifted over in some spots, so we've had to go slower than usual."

"We're giving Teddy a badly needed break," Logan said. "We'll do our best to make good time from here on out."

"That's fine." Chase paused for a moment, then said, "Stay safe, you two. We'll see you soon."

"Sounds good. Thanks, Chase." Jessica hit the

button to end the call. "Now he'll want the whole story once they pick us up."

He grimaced. "Sorry. I hate to say it was a knee-jerk reaction to him accusing me of crashing my plane."

"He knows you're a good pilot, Logan." She rolled her eyes and stroked Teddy's fur. "It wasn't that long ago that we rushed in to rescue him and his son, Eli, from the kidnappers on the Wind River Reservation."

He nodded. Chase Sullivan could be intimidating, but he was also a genuinely nice guy. Logan was glad to have been able to lend a hand when Chase needed it.

"I guess we should keep going." With a low groan, Jess stood. "Chase and Shane are going to beat us to the campground as it is."

"That's true." He stood as well. Teddy was the last to move. The dog lifted his head, huffed out a sigh, and lumbered to all fours. Then the K9 stretched for a long moment as if dragging out the break for as long as possible. Yet as soon as Jessica moved forward, Teddy straightened and trotted to keep up.

The dog had more personality than some of the people he knew. He let Jess set the pace, and they pushed forward for another hour.

"Poor Teddy," she said, when they stopped to rest.

"He's doing fine." Not that he was the dog expert she was. "I think he senses the end of the hike is near."

She gave Teddy some water, then shared the last of the water bottle with him. He gratefully downed what was left. He tucked the bottle into his pack, thinking about the end of their trip being a mile away. As much as he was glad they wouldn't have to spend another night camping on the mountain, he had to admit he would miss spending time with Jess. She was the best traveling companion he'd been with, and under better circumstances—like when someone wasn't trying to kill them—he'd love to do this again.

Jess only rested for five minutes. He was surprised when she rose. "Let's go. We're almost at the campground, right?"

"Yes." He glanced at Teddy, who seemed to be good to go. He double-checked their coordinates, then continued walking. It didn't take long for them to reach the outer edge of the campground.

"I don't see a car, do you?" Jess craned her neck as they walked along a rustic road past several empty campsites. "I can't imagine we beat Chase and Shane here."

He frowned, scanning the area. "The campground is large. I'm sure they're waiting in the main parking area."

She sighed. Teddy sniffed the campsites with interest. They walked for another half a mile when Teddy abruptly lifted his nose to the air and began to growl.

Logan's instincts went on full alert. He turned to scan the woods behind them, wondering if he'd been wrong about the gunman following them.

"What is it, Teddy?" Jess sounded nervous. "What caught your attention?"

Teddy stared intently into the woods to their right, then began to bark. The same sharp barks that had woken him from a sound sleep.

"Let's find cover." He reached for Jess's arm to pull her back.

"Jessica? Are you out there?" a male voice shouted above Teddy's barking. "We're here! We're coming!"

Logan continued pulling Jess toward a cluster of trees. Teddy continued to bark for a solid minute before suddenly stopping.

Chase and Shane came running up the trail toward them accompanied by their respective dogs, Chase's Norwegian Elkhound, Rocky, and Shane's German shepherd, Bryce. He shouldn't have been surprised to see that both men were armed with handguns. "What's going on?" Chase asked. "What caught Teddy's attention?"

"I'm not sure," Jess responded. "I don't see anyone."

Logan didn't see anyone either but wasn't reassured. The threat could have backed off when the cavalry had arrived.

Was it possible the same man who'd nearly stumbled into their campsite had been following them the entire time? And if so, why?

5

Teddy's growling was so unlike him that Jess turned to scan their surroundings. Rocky and Bryce were excited to see Teddy, and within seconds, the three dogs were playing.

Whatever had caught Teddy's attention must have moved on. Had Teddy alerted on a wild animal? Or had he caught the scent of a human threat?

Her K9 had sniffed the footprints near their camp beside the hunting shanty with interest, so she knew he'd remember the intruder. Yet it seemed improbable that the bad guy had followed them all this way. What would be the point? If he was armed, he could have taken them out of the picture at any time.

"Hey, Logan." Chase held out his hand. Logan took it. "Thanks for keeping Jess safe."

"Of course." Logan turned to greet her younger brother Shane too. "I feel bad about putting her in danger."

"I'm fine, thanks," she said curtly. "In fact, Teddy was the real hero. He scared the intruder away."

Chase arched a brow. "Let's head back to the SUVs. I'd like to understand exactly what happened."

She sighed. "Sure thing. Although if you don't mind, we'd love to stop for breakfast on the way home. All we've had so far is a couple of granola and protein bars, and after a five-mile hike, I'm famished."

"I wouldn't mind a second breakfast," Shane said with a grin. "We burned a lot of calories worrying about you."

"Yeah, that works," Chase agreed. "Anna would be upset if we didn't feed you both." Chase raised his voice. "Rocky, here!" His K9 ignored him.

Hiding a smile, Jess called to her dog. "Teddy, heel!" Her dog loped to her side.

"Come, Bryce," Shane added. The large shepherd obeyed his command too.

Rocky finally trotted to Chase's side, but only because his playmates had stopped playing with him. It was an ongoing source of entertainment for the siblings how Chase's K9 was so stubborn.

"If you don't behave, I'm trading you in for a new

model," Chase threatened, reaching over to scratch Rocky's ears.

The K9 wagged his tail as if knowing an empty promise when he heard one.

Jess knew Chase would never give up Rocky, especially now that his son, Elijah, and his new wife, Wynona, had settled in at the ranch. Eli loved that dog and had established a bond with the animal her brother would never break.

"We brought two SUVs." Shane gestured to her backpack as they headed up the trail to the parking lot. "We knew you'd have a lot of gear with you."

"Logan was prepared." She glanced at Logan, who hadn't said much since her brothers had joined them. "He had camping gear in the back of his plane. Oh, that reminds me." She frowned. "We need to get back to his plane soon. Not only did some idiot damage it, but we found a piece of a tail fin that could belong to our parents' plane."

"Wait, run that by me again?" Chase interrupted. "Why did someone shoot at the plane?"

"It's a long story." She sighed. "It might be better if we started at the beginning."

"I want to hear this," Shane protested. "Wait until we stop to get breakfast before you spill the details."

She knew Chase would drill them the moment they hit the road. As she stopped beside the SUVs, she noticed that her brothers had brought the two freshly painted ones, so there was no K9 Sullivan logo etched along the side. With a sense of relief, she shrugged off the backpack, dropping it to the ground. "Look, it's not a long story. Chase dropped a charter off at the base of Cedar Mountain. While circling back toward home, he spied a piece of plane debris. He came to the ranch and asked me if I wanted to go with him to pick it up."

"Without telling anyone your plan," Chase said with a narrow gaze.

"Yes, as I said, it was supposed to be a short trip. A couple of hours at most." She held Logan's green gaze for a moment, then continued. "We found the piece of debris. Logan landed in an open area nearby, and we hiked out to grab it. That's when the first shots were fired."

"Rifle shots," Logan said, filling in some details. "They sounded as if they came from a distance not a close range handgun."

"We ducked for cover." She picked up the story. "Logan ran out to get the plane part, and we headed into the woods. It was slow going without being on a trail, but we eventually got back to the plane. Logan took us up, and then the plane engine misfired. We believe because more shots were fired. If not for Logan's expertise, we may have crashed. He managed to land the plane, driving it into the brush. We grabbed our gear and disappeared back into the woods to avoid the gunman."

"A bullet struck the right wing," Logan added. "Took off a big enough chunk that made it difficult to keep the bird level."

"Had to have been another rifle shot," Shane said.

"Exactly our thought," she agreed. "And like I said, Logan had a bunch of camping gear on his plane. We spent the night near an old hunting shanty. Teddy barked like crazy early this morning. When we climbed out of the tent, we found a set of footprints about sixty yards or so from our camp."

"The tent was covered with snow, so I believe Teddy caught the guy off guard." Logan shrugged. "That's the only thing that makes sense. If he'd seen the tent and known we were inside . . ."

She winced at Shane's and Chase's grim expressions. "We don't know for sure he was armed. But yeah, Teddy's barking absolutely saved the day."

"Good boy," Shane murmured. "I'm glad you had Teddy with you."

"Oh yeah, one more thing." She glanced at Logan who gave her a tiny nod. "I almost forgot that Teddy alerted on a glove that was left behind by Logan's client."

Chase scowled. "Are you saying the guy who chartered the plane is dealing drugs?"

"That's our working theory, yes," Logan said somberly. "If I had known, I wouldn't have flown him to the Bighorns. But obviously, once someone started firing shots at us, we assumed Craig Benton is up to no good."

"If that's his real name," she added. "He paid Logan in cash, so we suspect he provided an alias."

"Well, that's not good," Shane muttered.

"We're fine, and that's all that matters." She didn't need Shane's doom and gloom. "Now that we suspect drugs are involved, Teddy can help locate them."

"I don't think that's a good idea." Logan looked over her shoulder toward Chase. "It's too dangerous. Law enforcement needs to take the lead on this moving forward."

She was annoyed at Logan's interference. "When exactly will Doug and Maya arrive home? Today, right? I know Doug's expertise as a former DEA agent would be helpful in uncovering the truth."

"Doug and Maya had a slight delay. They won't get to the ranch until later tonight," Chase said. "We can wait until tomorrow."

She didn't like the thought of waiting. "And what about Logan's plane? We can't just leave it there."

"It's fine," Logan said. "Thankfully, I have two other birds to use in the meantime. And who knows if I'll even get any charters in that time frame."

"We still need to get that piece of tail fin that we were forced to leave behind." She narrowed her gaze, willing Logan to support her on this. "I think we should head back tomorrow to repair the plane and to get the tail fin."

Chase lifted his hand to end the discussion. "I thought you wanted breakfast? It's time to hit the road."

She was hungry, so she let it go. For now. "Yeah, I do. And I would love some coffee too."

"Hop in." Chase nodded toward the SUV closest to them. "I'll put Rocky in the back. Teddy will have to share the backseat with you, sis."

She glanced at Logan. He avoided her gaze, focusing on shrugging out of his pack and setting it on the floor of the back seat. He put her backpack inside, too, then opened the passenger door to sit up front.

Shaking her head, she turned to Teddy. "Up."

Teddy gracefully jumped into the back of the SUV, pressing his nose against Rocky's crate screen. She climbed in beside him. She nearly moaned in relief. It felt so good to be off her feet.

If she wasn't such a wimp, she'd insist on heading out to get Logan's plane later that day. But she couldn't do it. Her body needed rest. And she knew convincing Logan and her siblings to head out again so soon would be impossible.

It bothered her to know Logan had been forced to leave his damaged plane in the woods. He hadn't complained, yet she felt responsible. She wished she knew what was going on, who Craig Benton was, and what drugs he'd transported.

As Chase pulled out of the campground parking lot, she drew Teddy across her lap. She buried her fingers in his fur, leaned her head back against the seat cushion, and closed her eyes.

Rest, then food. Uncovering the truth behind the drugs that had been carried to the mountains via Logan's plane would have to wait.

But not for too long. An image of Ella's face filled her mind. Ella was just one of hundreds of thousands who'd lost their lives to drug addiction. If Teddy could help eradicate the illegal drug trade in their small part of the state, she'd accept that mission.

No matter what.

LOGAN BATTLED fatigue as Chase took Highway 14 west toward Greybull. It was the soothing motion of the car that was doing him in. Well, that and the fact that they'd hiked well over twelve miles over the past fourteen hours.

"We'll head to Della's Diner for breakfast," Chase said, breaking into his thoughts.

"Sounds good." He blinked to keep himself awake and focused "My place isn't too far from there. I appreciate you dropping me off."

"It's no trouble." Chase glanced at him. "We're grateful at how well you looked after Jess."

He knew Chase was fishing for information. He glanced over his shoulder to see that Jessica had fallen asleep. So had Teddy. "We're friends, that's all. Besides, you know Jess would slug me if I tried anything."

"That's true." Chase grinned. "I also know you have too much respect for Jess to have tried anything."

He flushed and looked out the window. He knew his feelings for Jess weren't much of a secret. Yet he also knew nothing would ever come of it. Burned bridges around Ella's death had taken care of that. "Like I said, we're friends."

"Do you really think the gunman shot at you because you got too close to his drug stash?" He was grateful Chase changed the subject. "Seems rather drastic."

"That's the only thing that makes sense." He shrugged. "Think about it from Benton's viewpoint. I drop him off, then return a short while later, hiking through the woods in the general direction of where he was headed."

"Still seems like overkill," Chase muttered. "But I guess he could have been suspicious about the way you returned to the scene."

"I didn't expect him to try to crash the plane," Logan admitted. "I assumed the first shots were a warning to stay away. And it worked as we sure left in a hurry."

"Not your fault." Chase waved a hand. "I'm just glad you were able to land the plane."

"Me too." As they approached the town of Grey-bull, he straightened. Della's Diner was on the far east side of town. Now that they were close, his stomach rumbled loud enough for Chase to hear.

Greybull was smaller than Cody. Highway 14 merged with Highway 20 for a short distance before heading east again. Chase slowed and turned into the small parking lot of Della's Diner. Shane pulled in beside him.

"Wake up, Jess," Chase said.

"Huh?" Jess blinked, then ducked as Teddy tried to lick her face. "Wow, you got here fast."

Logan couldn't help but smile. Jess pushed Teddy off her lap to unlatch her seat belt. "I hope they don't mind dogs."

"They won't," Chase assured her. "I've been here before with Rocky."

Logan wasn't worried either. The Sullivans were well known across the state of Wyoming for their search and rescue efforts. Second only to the governor, the Sullivan family was treated like royalty.

A well-deserved reputation, he silently acknowledged.

Chase let Rocky out of the back. The three Sullivans let their dogs run wild for a few minutes, before calling them back. Logan followed them inside the restaurant. Every patron in the place turned to stare at them.

Three dogs and four people were a lot, he conceded.

"This way." A server with four menus escorted them to a round table in the back. Logan ended up sitting beside Jessica, who kept Teddy close to her side. "Coffee?"

"Yes, please," he and Jess answered in unison.

"We'll have some too," Chase added dryly.

The coffee was strong and hot, just the way Logan liked it. After placing their orders, he cradled his mug, grateful to be safe and warm.

"I was thinking that Logan should return to the ranch with us," Jessica said, breaking the silence.

He was so shocked by her offer he nearly spilled his coffee. "Oh, I really should head home. I need to find spare parts to repair my plane anyway."

"That's just it. We should pay for the parts." Jessica turned to her oldest brother. "Come on, Chase. You know we owe Logan this much."

"I don't mind reimbursing him for the plane parts," Chase agreed. "Not sure that means he needs to stay at the ranch."

She frowned, then shrugged. "I just feel like we should stick together."

Logan was touched by her offer, but he privately agreed with Chase. There was no reason for him to spend time on the ranch.

"How far is your damaged plane from the campground?" Shane asked. "It might be easier to get there by car and snowmobile than to fly another of your planes."

He nodded slowly. "That's true. And once I get the plane repaired, I can fly it out of there."

"Unless the gunman is still hanging around and waiting to take another shot at you," Jess said.

He shrugged, unable to argue her point.

"Let's hold off on planning a return trip just yet." Chase looked exasperated. "When we do decide to return, we'll need to take the local sheriff and maybe a couple of game wardens along in case there is more trouble."

Jess frowned, then nodded. "You're right. We need others as backup."

Their server arrived carrying a large tray stacked with large breakfast meals. Teddy lifted his head, no doubt latching on to the scent of bacon. After they'd been given their respective plates and their cups refilled with coffee, their server left them alone.

"I'd like to say grace," Jess said.

Chase looked surprised. "Go ahead then."

"Dear Lord Jesus, we thank You for keeping us safe in Your care last night and this morning. We ask You to bless this food and to continue to guide us on the path so that we might find these criminals and bring them to justice. Amen."

"Amen," Logan said. Chase and Shane exchanged a look before echoing the sentiment.

"I'm not sure bringing criminals to justice is our job," Chase pointed out once they dug into their meals. "We do search and rescue missions, not search and arrest."

"Even if that means turning your back on a drug dealer?" Jess asked. "Seriously?"

"We don't know for sure what Craig Benton is involved in." Logan spoke between bites. "We're assuming drugs because of Teddy's alert. But the guy could be poaching or doing something else entirely."

"Something bad enough to try to kill us," Jess fired back. "I highly doubt a poacher is going to risk killing two innocent people and a dog."

He sighed and took another bite of his farmer's

omelet. The food warmed his belly. "I'm just saying we shouldn't jump to conclusions."

"Logan has a point," Shane said. When Jess glared at him, he raised a hand. "I know Teddy is rarely wrong when it comes to finding drugs. But having drugs in your pocket for personal use and dealing them are two different things."

"You're all nuts," Jess muttered. "And if Doug were here, he'd agree with me on this."

They finished the rest of their meal in silence. Logan knew that no matter what he said, Jess would insist on being included in the trip back up the mountain.

When their server brought their bill, he dug in his pocket for some cash to pay for his meal. Chase waved him off. "Put it away. We've got this."

Sensing that arguing was useless, he let it go. The Sullivans were known not to accept more than a bag of dog food for their services, and he'd always assumed they'd gotten some sort of inheritance from their parents.

Yet that didn't mean he shouldn't pay his way.

They all stood and began pulling on their winter coats, hats, and gloves. The dogs jumped to their feet, raring to go. Logan could feel the curious gazes as they trooped toward the front door.

"Nothing like drawing a whole lot of attention," he said to Shane. "Does this happen all the time?"

Shane lifted a brow and shrugged. "Didn't notice."

Because they're the closest thing to royalty around here. He shook his head and stood watching as the three Sullivan siblings sent their dogs out for a quick romp around the restaurant before calling them back. Even Teddy, who had to be exhausted from their earlier trek down the mountain, eagerly played along with Rocky and Bryce.

As usual, Rocky was the last one to head over when called. Logan tried to hide his amusement at Chase's frustration.

"Rocky, heel!" He shouted the command loud enough to be heard all the way to Cody. After staring Chase down for a long minute, Rocky relented and trotted over to the SUV.

"That dog is something else," he said in a low voice to Jess as Chase managed to get Rocky settled in the back crate area of the SUV. "I thought all K9s were well trained?"

"Elkhounds are a different breed." She grinned. "More independent than most and not as anxious to please their handlers. Somehow, I don't think Chase will get another Elkhound once Rocky retires from SAR duty. But since Rocky is only five, he has many years of fighting with that dog ahead of him."

Logan held the back door open for Jess and Teddy. Soon, they were back on the highway. His log cabin home was only another three miles down the road on the outskirts of town. He'd purchased the property after his mother died. His dad had left when he was just a kid, and Logan had no real memory of the guy. Other than the scent of cigarette smoke. When Logan passed a smoker, he thought only briefly of the man who'd walked away without looking back.

His mom had done well enough without him, working at a small motel and then buying the place when the owner retired. Logan had felt bad selling the motel after she'd died, but his mother had always encouraged his love of flying, so he was sure she'd appreciate his desire to purchase a property with a built-in airstrip. Not to mention an airplane hangar. The previous owner had left an old plane behind, and Logan had pretty much rebuilt the engine from scratch to get her back in flying condition.

That was how he ended up with three planes. *Well, two now*, he thought with a sigh. He hadn't had time to examine the damage too closely after the near crash landing. He hoped it wouldn't take too much to get the bird airborne.

A few minutes later, Chase pulled into his driveway. He quickly pushed his door open. "Thanks again."

"Back at you," Chase answered. "We appreciate everything you did for Jess."

"Jess can speak for herself," she said irritably. Then she sighed. "I am grateful you were with me last night. And I hope to see you again soon."

"Sure thing." Logan told himself Jess didn't mean that the way it sounded. She was more concerned about tracking the potential drug dealer than seeing him again on a personal level. And that was fine. He needed to focus on repairing his plane anyway.

He grabbed his oversized backpack from the rear seat and slung it over his shoulder. "Take care." He gave Jess a nod and turned to head toward the airplane hangar. No reason to haul the pack into the house. He'd have to go through it to rearrange stuff, but he wanted to be sure he had the pack stored in his second favorite plane for his next trip.

Obviously, it had been a good thing he and Jess had been able to use the tent and other camping gear last night.

He was about halfway to the hangar when he heard the sharp crack of gunfire. Seconds later, he felt the impact of a bullet striking his backpack. It was enough to throw him off balance. He instinctively dropped to his knees while digging his gun from his pocket.

"Logan!" Jessica's shout echoed around him. It was quickly followed by the roaring of the SUV engine. He frantically searched the section of woods located just north of his house, the most logical location for a gunman to hide.

"Get in!" Jess sounded angry now. "Hurry!"

He wasn't sure that was the best move, but he feared if he didn't go to the car, she'd rush toward him, placing herself in harm's way. Without giving himself too much time to think it through, he leaped to his feet and used the backpack to shield his head and neck as he ran toward the SUV.

Jess had the back door open. He didn't hesitate to dive inside. Without waiting for him to get situated, or even to get the door closed, Chase put the SUV in reverse and shot out of the driveway.

He finally managed to shove the backpack to the floor, leaning forward to grab the door handle to close it. Chase was still driving as fast as possible away from his home.

"Did you see who shot at you?" Chase demanded.

Dazed, he shook his head. He belatedly realized Teddy was sitting up in the passenger seat beside Chase. Surprised, he glanced at Jess. "No. I only heard the shot and felt the bullet strike the backpack."

"What?" Jessica's blue eyes widened in horror. "He just missed hitting you?"

He nodded and bent over to examine the backpack. There was a round hole on one side where the bullet had clearly struck and a larger frayed open area on the other side. An exit wound, so to speak.

"That was too close," Jess muttered. "Way too close."

"Yeah." He sat back, his thoughts whirling. They hadn't rushed their trip back from the mountain. They'd stopped to talk, then had stopped for breakfast at the Della's Diner.

Meanwhile, the gunman had lain in wait for him to get home. This was the third attempt to kill him, if the first shooting hadn't been a simple warning.

Three shootings within twenty-four hours.

Craig Benton had to be the man responsible.

6

Jess leaned forward and tapped her brother's shoulder to get Chase's attention. "We need to take Logan someplace safe."

"Not the ranch," Logan quickly interjected. "I don't want to bring danger to the rest of your family."

Chase's grim expression revealed his internal debate about their next steps. She didn't blame him for being concerned about his wife and young son. Putting Eli in harm's way was not an option. She nodded. "I agree, not the ranch. Maybe a hotel in Cody?"

"I don't like this," Chase muttered. "What in the world is going on?"

She didn't much like it either. Seeing the path of the bullet going through Logan's backpack was sobering. If the shot had been a few inches in the other direction, it would have torn through Logan's torso.

Killing him.

"I wish I knew. A hotel works." Logan scowled. "But I think Jess is in danger too."

She wanted to discount that possibility but couldn't. For one thing, she'd been with Logan on the mountain when the idiot had fired at them. And she'd been on the plane, too, when they'd nearly crashed. This most recent attempt may have been aimed at Logan, but she had no doubt the killer had planned to turn his attention on her next.

Why, she wasn't sure. Was she a target only because she'd been with Logan?

"Fine." She tried not to sigh. "Teddy and I can stay with you at the hotel for a while. But this shooting only adds credence to our theory of Craig Benton being involved with drugs. Obviously, Benton was able to figure out where you live."

"What about you, Jess?" Chase met her gaze in the rearview. "Do you think the shooter knows who you are?"

She shrugged and glanced at Logan. "If he's new to the area, probably not. Teddy was wearing his SAR vest, but this guy may not realize he's part of the Sullivan K9 crew. Good thing you used the two

SUVs without our family logo embossed along the sides."

"I never should have done that in the first place," Chase groused. "Considering you had Teddy with you, he may know about the ranch."

"I picked Benton up from Cheyenne to fly him to his requested destination within the Bighorns." Logan grimaced. "He gave me the coordinates and looked around with interest as we flew. If I had to guess, he's been to the location before. Everyone knows the Sullivans, so I think we have to assume he does too."

Chase sighed and rubbed the back of his neck. "Yeah, okay. I'll go along with using a hotel in Cody for now and then figure out our next steps."

A phone rang. Not hers, and when she glanced at Logan, he shook his head. Then she saw Shane's name on the dashboard media screen. Chase pressed a button on his steering wheel to answer. "Hey, Shane. New plan."

"Ya think?" Shane's voice dripped with sarcasm. "What happened back there?"

"Someone took a shot at Logan. Probably the same guy who tried to shoot down his plane," Chase said. "We're heading to Cody. If you want to peel off to return to the ranch, that's fine."

"Not happening," Shane said bluntly. "If anyone

should peel off, it's you. You have a wife and son to take care of."

"I'm aware," Chase said dryly.

"You'll have to leave one of these SUVs at the hotel for us," she said. "In case we need to go on the move."

Both Chase and Shane were silent for a long moment. "Maybe I should stay with Jess and Logan too," Shane said.

"Not necessary," she quickly interjected. "Three people and two dogs will attract too much attention. Logan and I can pretend to be on vacation with our family pet."

"I agree about three adults and two dogs attracting attention," Logan said. "It was a bit alarming how everyone stared at us at the restaurant."

"I think it's best to let Jessica and Logan stay at the hotel with Teddy." Chase's firm tone ended the discussion. "Shane, we'll stop by to have a chat with the Cody police department before we head to the ranch. I know their department is small, and they have a rookie cop who barely looks old enough to shave, but we'll convince them to keep an eye on things at the Elk Lodge."

She arched a brow. "Is that where we're staying?"

Chase nodded. "Unless you have a better idea. I'll arrange for a suite."

"That's not going to look like a couple on vacation," she pointed out.

"Get a single king bedroom suite and I'll sleep on the sofa," Logan said. "We'll pretend to be on our honeymoon."

Hearing Logan say "our honeymoon" sent a shiver of awareness down her spine. A ridiculous response to a guy who'd dated her best friend. Okay, yes, that was eight years ago, but she wasn't interested in him on a personal level.

Only as a friend, nothing more.

"A honeymoon to the Elk Lodge?" Shane laughed. "That's a good one."

She sighed. There were times her family got on her nerves. "For some people, a suite at the Elk Lodge would be a luxury."

"She's right." Chase once again put an end to the discussion.

"Okay, meet you there." Shane ended the call.

She used her phone to search for a suite at the Elk Lodge. To her surprise, there was a king bedroom suite available. But she didn't book it, knowing that would require a credit card. One that could possibly be traced. She eyed Chase in the rearview. "Are you thinking we should pay in cash for the room?"

"Yeah, I'll take care of it." Her brother frowned. "I can only hope the clerk can keep it quiet."

She nodded. Logan was right. Everyone in Cody

knew the Sullivan family. But so did the people in Greybull. In fact, she couldn't think of a city nearby where her last name wouldn't garner recognition.

Teddy rested his head on the center console and slept as they drove. She wouldn't have minded another nap either, but between the coffee and the gunfire, adrenaline still buzzed through her bloodstream.

"Do you really think the local police can help keep us safe?" Logan eyed Chase. "I seem to recall one of the cops getting arrested a few months ago."

Jess knew the story, although the family had tried to keep their name out of it. "Yeah, I heard about that too. But I think the other cops are decent, right, Chase?"

"Yes." Chase answered without hesitation. "And I'm sure they'll help keep an eye on the Elk Lodge while you and Jess are staying there."

Logan fell silent, and she could understand his concern. It seemed like eons had passed since they'd felt safe.

And somehow, she didn't anticipate feeling safe even while hiding out in the hotel suite.

"At least we'll be warm and dry." She managed a light smile. "And there's the added bonus of room service."

"That's a step up from camping in the snow for sure," Logan agreed.

His comment only reminded her of how she'd slept with her head resting on his chest. Averting her gaze, she reminded herself that they were fully dressed and nothing inappropriate had happened.

It was well over an hour later when Chase pulled into the parking lot of the Elk Lodge. It sported a rustic motif, but it was also the nicest hotel in the city. Perfect for their pretend honeymoon.

"I should have insisted on staying at a resort in Jackson for our honeymoon," she teased as Chase slid out from behind the wheel. "They have some fancy ones there."

"Very funny." Her brother scowled. "Stay here. I'll be back soon."

Teddy lifted his head to look around, seemingly confused that they weren't back at the ranch. She grabbed her pack from the floor at her feet and stuffed her phone into the front pocket. "I have a charging cord if you need one."

"That would be great." Logan gestured to his overstuffed pack. "My gear is for surviving outdoors. No phone cords needed."

"Makes sense." She wondered why things were suddenly so awkward between them. "I hope we can get the local cops to head back out to the mountain soon."

"All in good time." He gave a nonchalant shrug.

"Hey, open up." Shane tapped on her window. She obliged by opening her door. "Do you want my keys?"

"Ah, sure." She took the key fob for his SUV. "Thanks."

A minute later, Chase returned with two room keys. She slid out of the SUV. "Come, Teddy."

"You're in a suite on the ground floor, room 1008," Chase explained. "There's a side exit down the hall, so you can take Teddy outside as needed without having to go through the lobby."

"That's great." She accepted her key. Logan took the second one. "And they're going to keep our name secret?"

"I put you down as Mr. and Mrs. Lyle Kirkpatrick, here celebrating your honeymoon." Chase grinned when Logan scowled at his fake name. "The clerk didn't seem to care who was staying in the room since I slipped him a little extra to keep quiet. Oh, and I paid enough to cover room service and any other amenities for the next two days."

She rolled her eyes. "Hotel clerks are not supposed to give out the names of their guests. Whether you pay them a little extra or not."

"Yeah, well, if they slip up, it won't matter." Chase's smile faded. "Stay safe, okay? Shane and I will be in touch after we chat with the local police."

"Thanks, Chase." Logan glanced at her, then

added, "I'm armed. Hopefully, we won't be in a position where I need to use my gun."

"I pray that won't be necessary too," Chase agreed.

"Me three." She shouldered her pack. "Come, Teddy." She paused, then glanced at her brother. "I assume we can access the side entrance with our keys?"

"Yep. And that's a good thought to head in that way," Chase agreed. "There's extra dog food and other supplies in Shane's SUV."

"I know. Thanks." She headed toward the back of the building with Teddy trotting at her side. Logan stayed back, letting her take the lead.

The suite was nicer than she'd expected. There was a small living area along with a kitchenette. Moving forward, she poked her head through the doorway leading to the bedroom.

"Are you sure about sleeping on the sofa?" She glanced at Logan over her shoulder.

"Yep." The corner of his mouth tugged up in a grin. "I can always use the sleeping bag if needed."

"Right." She stripped off her winter coat, hat, and gloves. Raking her fingers through her long blond hair, she wished she had a toiletry kit so she could take a shower. The suite was much larger than the tent but felt oddly more intimate. She told herself to stop letting her imagination run amok. There was no reason to be worried.

They were safe here.

Yet she had a feeling that being cooped up with Logan for the rest of the day would be more difficult than hiking through the woods while trying to avoid being struck by a bullet.

LOGAN SET his pack up along the side of the room, the gaping bullet hole seeming to mock him. He wasn't sure that staying here with Jess was the right move.

But he couldn't come up with a decent alternative either.

First and foremost, he wanted her to be safe. And for now, this seemed the best way to accomplish that task. Even if it meant staying in a hotel room together.

He stood, looking everywhere but at Jess. As he shed his coat, hat, and gloves, he tried to think about how the police would manage to track Craig Benton. Especially if the guy used a fake name.

He had a bad feeling they wouldn't have much success without help from the Sullivans. Specifically, Jessica and Teddy.

Jess ducked into the bedroom long enough to

drop her backpack, then returned to the living room. She seemed ill at ease too. This situation was hardly normal for either of them.

She sighed. "This is going to be a long day. I'm not used to having nothing to do."

"I hear you on that." He turned and headed toward the kitchenette. "More coffee?"

"That would be great." She sat on the sofa and called Teddy to her side. The dog stretched out on the floor near her feet and promptly went to sleep. Shaking her head, she stroked her hand over Teddy's fur. "Poor Teddy. He is one tuckered pup."

"He deserves to rest." After making the coffee, he leaned back against the counter, facing her across the room. "I don't think you should volunteer Teddy's services to law enforcement. I understand he's a good tracker, but it's safer to let the game warden and the local police track down Benton."

She snorted and shook her head. "You must realize they won't find him without our help. Oh, I'm sure they'd give it a good try, but you said yourself that you didn't see a cabin or dwelling near the location where you dropped Benton off. The landing area is a good starting point, but without Teddy's nose, I doubt they'll find anything."

"I also said I wasn't really looking for a cabin." He didn't like sounding defensive. "It could be there."

"I'm sure if there had been a cabin, you'd have noticed." She made an exasperated sound and held his gaze for a long minute. "Come on, Logan. Doesn't the fact that Ella died of a drug overdose mean anything to you?"

He flinched as if she'd slapped him across the face. "I told you; I had no idea Ella was doing drugs. She certainly never used them around me."

Was that a flash of regret in her blue eyes? He wasn't sure. She shrugged and looked away. "I just think that since we both cared about Ella that we'd want to do our part in getting rid of anyone profiting from selling drugs. It feels like the least we can do."

He stared down at his boots for a moment. "Yeah, of course I care about getting rid of drugs. And those dealing them." He lifted his gaze to hers. "I'm the one who agreed to fly Benton to the mountain. That means I'm the reason we're in this mess. Putting yourself and Teddy in danger isn't going to bring Ella back."

"I never said it would. But the truth is that Teddy is a great narcotics dog." She stroked the dog's fur again. "You know as well as I do that this K9 is our best chance to find Benton and whoever else he's working with. Especially since I'm pretty sure Teddy has locked on the gunman's scent. Between him and the drugs, Teddy should lead us straight toward him."

He knew that was true. He didn't much like it, but Jess was stubborn enough to do whatever she wanted.

With blatant disregard for the consequences.

He'd hoped Chase might talk her out of it. But from what he could tell, her older brother was more likely to join in the search than to hold his sister back.

The coffeemaker gurgled behind him. He turned and poured two mugs, bringing one to Jessica.

"Thanks." She cradled the mug in her hands, her gaze turning thoughtful. "I hate to admit it, but I never saw Ella doing drugs either. And I thought we were good friends. I know I blamed you for not realizing what was going on, but that was wrong of me. I should have noticed if she was under the influence."

He sat on the opposite end of the sofa, reassured by her comment. It was no secret Jess had blamed him for Ella's overdose. And he'd understood her concern. As Ella's boyfriend, it would be reasonable to think he'd have known something.

But he'd been just as horrified as everyone else when Ella's parents found her dead the morning after their breakup. "She must have hidden it well. Everyone was surprised by her death."

She nodded and sipped the coffee. "Her brother,

Ethan, was shocked. I remember asking him about it."

That made him frown. "Ethan? He was two years older than Ella. I'm surprised you were friends with him."

"He's Chase's age." She shrugged. "We went out on a few dates. It was nothing serious, though. And it didn't last."

There was no reason on earth for him to be jealous of Ethan Dover. Jessica had a right to date anyone she wanted. Or to not date anyone, like him.

He told himself to get a grip and tried to sound casual. "Ethan was already living on his own while I was dating Ella."

He didn't like rehashing his painful past or the mistakes he'd made when it came to going out with Ella. The night of their argument played over and over in his mind. He debated telling Jess, then decided against it. She didn't need more ammunition to use against him. And even if they had argued, that didn't mean he was responsible for her drug overdose.

Was he?

"You weren't friends with Ethan?"

He shook his head. "I doubt I said more than five words to him."

"Yeah, well, that kinda makes sense. Ella and Ethan didn't always get along. Ethan told me Ella was spoiled, but I was a loyal friend and defended her. But in hindsight, maybe he was right. She seemed to get whatever she wanted. Her parents were rather liberal with giving her money." She set her mug of coffee aside. "I guess it doesn't matter. As you said, nothing will bring Ella back. But this is about other kids that live here too. I can't stand the thought of Benton and others making a profit off people's weaknesses."

"I don't like it either." He sighed, knowing there was no way he'd win the fight. Jess would take Teddy back to the mountainside to search for Benton or the drugs he must have been carrying, and there was nothing he could do to stop her.

"Oh, I almost forgot." Jess abruptly stood and disappeared into the bedroom. Teddy woke up, lifted his head, but didn't get to his feet. She returned with the phone charger, plugging it into an outlet that was built into the bottom of a lamp sitting on the end table beside her. "Hand me your phone."

He pulled it from his pocket, intending to pass it to her, but then stopped. "It just occurred to me that Benton has my phone number. And that I have his too."

She stared at him for a long moment. "Maybe you should try calling him."

He hesitated, then scrolled through his recent

calls to find the number. He pressed the button on the screen and shouldn't have been surprised to hear the mechanical voice informing him the number was no longer in service. He frowned and lowered his phone. "Must have been a burner."

"Yeah. And if he got rid of the burner, then it's not likely he kept your number. I guess that's one problem we don't have to worry about." She held out her hand. "Let me charge it up for you."

He gave it to her and tried not to imagine Craig Benton having the resources to track his phone. If the guy was still in the mountains, he wouldn't be concerned.

But someone had taken shots at him at his home in Greybull. And there was plenty of cell service in town.

Teddy lumbered to his feet, stretched for a long leisurely moment, then gazed up at Jessica. She nodded as if understanding the K9's unspoken request. "Do you want to go outside?"

At the word *outside*, the dog trotted toward the door, then glanced back at her, his dark-brown eyes expectant. Jess laughed and reached for her coat.

"Okay, I hear you, Teddy."

"Hang on, I'll come with you." He grabbed his jacket.

She arched a brow. "Pretty sure I can handle it."

"Yeah, I know." He patted his pocket to make

sure he still had the room key. "But a wise woman once told me it was better to stick together."

She chuckled and reached for the door handle. "Gosh, she sounds super smart."

"More like a smart aleck." He followed her down the hall toward the door at the end of the hall that led directly outside. Chase was the smart one to ask for a room on the ground floor. It was something he wouldn't have considered. Then again, he hadn't had a dog since he was a kid. His mother hadn't been interested in having a pet, and since she worked long hours, he understood the real reason behind her refusal to consider getting a dog was because she couldn't handle the additional stress.

Life as a single mother had been hard enough.

Jess stepped outside, the bright sunlight washing over her. He stood back, watching her with the dog. There was a park located across the street from the hotel. She headed that way with Teddy to find an area that would have grass if it wasn't for the recent snowfall. As it was, the sun was melting the snow leaving patches of grass poking through. That was spring in Wyoming for you. The weather changed on a dime. Either from good to bad, like the unexpected snowstorm late yesterday or from bad to good, like the sunshine today.

"Get busy, Teddy." She waved a hand. "Get busy!"

He had to smile when the dog sniffed, lifted his leg to pee, then sniffed again and made a complete circle before getting down to the task at hand. "I bet Rocky doesn't go to the bathroom on command."

"You'd win that bet." She shook her head and dug in her coat pocket for a baggie. She crossed over to clean up after her dog. "It's never dull watching Chase and Rocky battle for the upper hand."

He scanned their surroundings, reassured that the people of Cody, Wyoming, were busy with their usual routines. He didn't see anything suspicious, but then again, there were more people milling about than usual. The mild weather tended to bring people out in droves. Soon he'd be inundated with tourist requests.

It would be nice to have his plane repaired before then.

Teddy suddenly lifted his head and pricked his ears forward. Then he growled low in his throat.

"What is it?" Jess glanced around nervously. "What's wrong, Teddy?"

The dog abruptly darted deeper into the park, barking furiously now. It took Logan a minute to realize Teddy must have scented the gunman.

"Teddy, heel!" Jess's tone was frantic. And he knew she was worried the gunman would shoot and kill her dog. "Teddy!"

The dog continued to bark but abruptly stopped near some playground equipment.

As he and Jess caught up to Teddy, a crack of gunfire rang out. Not a rifle this time, he noted. A handgun.

"Jess! Down!" He threw himself toward her, hoping to cover her with his body. She had bent over her K9 to protect him too. He mentally braced himself for another round of gunfire and for the impact of a bullet.

How had the gunman found them there?

7

———

Curling her body over Teddy's, Jessica's heart thundered in her chest. Teddy had caught the scent of the gunman!

Chaos erupted around them. She lifted her head, hoping to see the gunman, but all she saw were people running around, screaming in fear and panic.

Teddy stopped growling and barking, which made her think the gunman must have left the scene. No surprise he wouldn't stick around.

"Are you hurt?" Logan asked in a low voice.

"I don't think so." She took a moment to run her hands over Teddy's fur. His black coat would make it difficult to see an injury. Thankfully, her K9 appeared unharmed. "We're okay. You?"

"Fine." His clipped tone said otherwise. "Let's

get closer to the playground equipment to wait for the police to arrive."

She turned her head to look up at him. Logan's green eyes were far too close. "It might be better to head back to the hotel."

"Not yet." He eased upright, giving her a little room to breathe. "I'm not sure we can stay at the Elk Lodge after this."

That made her frown. "There's no reason to think the hotel is compromised. Teddy didn't alert on the gunman's scent right away. We were in the park for several minutes before he began to growl."

A flicker of uncertainty darkened his gaze. "I don't know. I'm concerned the gunman may have been watching us."

"How?" She managed to stand. "Come, Teddy. This way." She led the dog toward the playground. There was a platform over a slide that offered some protection. But she was convinced the gunman was long gone.

As if to prove her point, the wail of police sirens filled the air. She briefly considered asking Teddy to find the gunman but quickly decided against it. She couldn't put her K9 in harm's way.

She wasn't a cop. She just happened to have a dog smart enough to alert them to danger.

"We need to call Chase to let him know about this," Logan said as the squad arrived. Two officers emerged from the vehicle and stood, glancing around. She recognized the older of them as Burt Jones. The younger guy must have been the new rookie they'd been hearing about.

A replacement for the dirty cop who'd been arrested back in January.

"Over here!" She waved her arm to get Burt's attention. She would have stepped forward, but Logan grabbed her arm.

"Let them come to us," he said.

Logan was being a bit overprotective, yet they had been targeted by this gunman far too often over the past twenty-four hours. Burt gave her a nod of recognition as he approached.

"Jessica. Do you know something about the report of gunfire that was called in?"

"Yeah, we do." She glanced at Logan who didn't seem to recognize the officers. "Do you know Logan Fletcher? He owns Fletcher's Flying."

"I'm not sure we've been formally introduced." Logan offered his hand, and both Burt and the rookie shook it.

"I'm Officer Jones, and this is Officer Jeff Riley." Burt looked from Logan back to her. "Don't tell me you were the target of this nutjob?"

"More likely I was," Logan said. "But I'm sure he wouldn't have held back from killing Jess either. It's a long story."

Burt hiked a brow. "Can't wait to hear it."

Another squad pulled up next to the first. Jess recognized Officer Rotterdam and the newly promoted Sergeant Wayne Carter. They rushed over to join them.

"What happened?" Wayne demanded.

"Look, do you think we could talk about this at the police station?" Logan asked. "I'd like Jessica and Teddy to be safe."

She could speak for herself, but Wayne quickly nodded. "I'll take you to the station to get your statements." Wayne turned to his officers. "You three spread out and search for the gunman and/or shell casings. The calls that came in through dispatch were rather vague. Guy wearing black was all they agreed on."

"Wait, I've been cross-training Teddy to find shell casings," she said. "I can ask him to search for gold."

"Not until we know the place is secure," Logan said, before Wayne could respond. He shot her an exasperated look. "That guy may not have gone very far."

"Even with four cops here?" She shook her head. "I don't think he's stupid enough to stick around. And really, Teddy's nose will work better than trying to scan the ground looking for the casing."

"She's right," Wayne agreed. "Let's have her dog

do his thing, then we'll head down to the police station."

Logan didn't look happy as he threw up his hands. "Fine. Let's just hope this guy isn't hiding nearby."

"Teddy would have alerted us to that if he was." She turned to her dog, who was looking up at her with his dark-brown eyes. "Are you ready to work?" she asked with enthusiasm. The trick with training K9s was to make every search effort a game. "Search for gold. Gold, Teddy. Search for gold!"

Her K9 lifted his head and began to test the air with his nose. Then he lowered his snout to the ground and began to cross the park. She quickly followed.

Logan and Wayne came along as well. Despite her confidence in Teddy's ability to scent the gunman, Jess swept a cautious gaze over the area. It was disconcerting to realize the gunman had been here just a few minutes earlier.

And how was it that he'd come across them? Cody wasn't a big city, but the town wasn't that small either. As the fifth largest city in the state, Cody had about ten thousand residents. The fact that the gunman happened to be there in the park at the same time she'd taken Teddy for a walk couldn't have been a coincidence.

But how had he found them? By locating one of their phones in some way?

She shivered and tried to focus on Teddy. Her K9 was trotting faster now, his nose along the ground as he headed toward a small, wooded area.

"Hold on, Jess," Wayne called. "Stay back. I don't want you to mess up a potential crime scene."

She eased to a stop but didn't take her gaze off Teddy. The dog slowed to sniff with interest near a large tree. Then he pawed at something in the snow.

"Find gold," she said encouragingly.

Teddy sat and let out a sharp bark. Ignoring Wayne's order to stay back, she moved forward, careful not to get too close to the crisscrossing of boot prints in the snow. She circled around to approach from the side.

That's when she spotted it. A shell casing embedded in the snow.

"Good boy, Teddy!" She praised her dog and reached into her pocket for the small brown stuffed moose. Each of the Sullivans had chosen a different toy to use as a reward for a job well done. She turned and tossed the moose up into the air, away from the crime scene.

Teddy nimbly darted forward to grab the toy before it hit the ground. Then he shook his head and ran around with the moose in his mouth.

"That dog is amazing," Wayne praised. "He found the shell casing faster than we would have."

She nodded. Logan still didn't look happy as he surveyed the area. "So the shooter was standing here when he fired at us." He turned to look beyond the playground area. "It's a straight shot, but too far to be accurate with a handgun."

"How do you know he used a handgun?" she asked.

"The sound was different from the rifle." Logan waved a hand. "I also think that using a long gun in town like this would have attracted too much attention."

"Logan's right, this is definitely a nine-millimeter shell casing." Wayne used his gloved hand to place it in an evidence bag. Then he pulled out his phone. "I don't see any clear footprints here, but he left a path from where he entered and exited the park."

Jess noticed the double sets of footprints Wayne had noted. The cop moved forward to take several pictures, before turning back to her. "This will help, although having an eyewitness who can describe this guy would be even better."

"I have a possible suspect," Logan said. "He gave me the name Craig Benton, but I'm sure that's an alias."

"Let's get you two, and the dog of course, back to

the station," Wayne said. "I think it's better if I hear this story from the beginning."

"My brothers Chase and Shane may have already spoken to the police chief," she said as she held out her hand for the stuffed moose. Teddy regurgitated the toy into her palm, his tail wagging as if he wanted to play the search game again.

"Well, if they did, the boss hasn't clued the rest of us in yet," Wayne said. "And I still need your statements for the record."

"Of course." She glanced at Logan, who nodded. "We're ready."

Wayne gave instructions to the three officers who would stay behind, then turned to head back to the squad. Logan sat up front, leaving her and Teddy to sit in the back. As she sat behind the partition, Jess realized this was the first time she'd ever been inside the back of a police car. At least she wasn't under arrest.

Stroking Teddy's fur, she tried to think about where they'd go once this interview was over. If her theory about the cell phone being tracked was correct, then Logan was right about the Elk Lodge being compromised.

And that meant the only way to be safe was to go completely off-grid. Maybe even to the point of leaving her family out of their plans moving forward.

Logan was relieved to head into the police station located near the center of town. The footprints leading away from the shell casing indicated the shooter had fled, but that didn't mean the guy had gone far.

With a good set of binoculars, the gunman could have easily taken up a position in a car parked nearby, watching them the entire time.

Waiting for another opportunity to strike.

"Please, have a seat." Sergeant Wayne Carter gestured to a pair of chairs positioned across a desk in the tiny office.

He and Jess did as he asked, and Teddy stretched out at Jessica's feet. Logan noticed the dog was never far from her side, offering another layer of protection.

But even a dog as protective as Teddy couldn't stop a bullet. This shooting, on the heels of the others, concerned him.

"If you don't mind starting at the beginning?" Wayne suggested.

He nodded and gave the background information as succinctly as possible. Craig Benton chartering the plane, seeing the piece of tail fin while he was leaving the area, then heading to the Sullivan ranch to pick up Jess. Wayne looked surprised to learn that Teddy had alerted to the scent of drugs on his plane.

"Drugs, huh?" Wayne sat back in his chair. "We've seen an increase in drug overdoses recently. The hospital has put out an alert and have supplied multiple doses of Narcan for our officers."

"Which drug specifically?" Jessica asked. "Meth? Heroin? Cocaine? Fentanyl?"

"Fentanyl has been the biggest concern," Wayne said. "Will your dog alert on any type of drug?"

"Yes, he's been trained to find them all." She reached down to stroke Teddy's fur. "We've even included the chemicals that are used to make synthetic drugs like fentanyl. When we go out on a search, I use the term peppers. That way nobody else knows what we're searching for."

"I see." Wayne nodded thoughtfully. "Okay, so back to your story. Teddy alerted on the scent of drugs that you believe were transported to the Bighorn Mountains by this Craig Benton guy."

"Yes. Benton lost a glove on the plane. Teddy found it. The drug scent may have been on that article of clothing." He shrugged, then continued the story. "We hiked out to where the plane part was located when someone fired shots at us using a rifle." He explained his theory that Benton might have assumed they'd returned to the area to find him, rather than picking up a piece of tail fin. It was ironic how his attempt to help the Sullivan family with information on their parents' plane crash had ended up putting Jessica in the middle of danger. "We returned to the plane to fly out, but he fired again, damaging the plane so that I had to make a crash landing."

He had Sergeant Carter's full attention now. "You're both lucky to be alive."

"Yep." He glanced at Jessica, knowing she wouldn't believe in luck so much as having faith in God watching over them. "Anyway, we hiked through the woods away from the plane, heading southwest. We camped in my tent overnight, and Teddy woke us the following morning growling and barking. We found a pair of tracks in the snow within sixty yards of our campsite."

"But the perp didn't shoot at you?" Wayne asked.

"No. The tent was covered in a layer of snow." He glanced at Jess again, then shrugged. "All I can figure is that he must not have realized we were camping there until Teddy created a ruckus."

"Go on," Wayne encouraged.

He finished the story, explaining about the gunfire at his home, and then this final attempt here in Cody. As he finished, it occurred to Logan that these incidents had crossed several jurisdictions. The mountains, which was probably federal land, the town of Greybull, and now Cody.

"I can see why the chief hasn't said much to us," Wayne muttered. "Everything up until this recent incident isn't our responsibility."

"Except now it does impact your department." Jessica's tone was sharp. "This guy followed us from the mountains, through Greybull, and here to Cody. We're going to need help from law enforcement to find and arrest this guy. Your cops and others will need to work together on this."

"Yeah, I get that." Wayne raked his hand over his hair. "But let's be honest, this is more of a federal case than a local one. I need to call the FBI offices in Cheyenne to see what they think."

Logan didn't like the way Wayne sounded as if he were passing the buck. "And how long will that take?"

The sergeant shrugged. "Can you describe Benton for me?"

He grimaced. "I hate to say it, but he was rather average. White guy, about five ten, maybe weighed one eighty pounds. He wore a hat, but I could tell he had dark hair. Brown, not black. Brown eyes too."

Wayne made notes, but Logan could tell the description was far from helpful.

"I would know him if I saw him again," he said. "Unfortunately, this guy has been smart enough not to get too close."

"Teddy will also recognize him," Jess said. "He alerted us to the gunman just before he fired at us."

"Okay, is there anything else you can think of that will help us find him?" Wayne asked.

"He had a lot of cash on him when he paid me," Logan said. "I figured he was rich, not that he was a drug dealer."

Wayne made another note. "I'll discuss our next steps with the chief. Oh, and I need your contact information."

"We won't be using our phones from this point forward," Jessica said. "They're in the Elk Lodge. I'd like your officers to get our gear out, though. I have a lot of Teddy's things in there that I need back."

"That's no problem, but why are you getting rid of your phones?" Wayne scowled. "I can't imagine Benton can track them."

"I don't know of any other way he could have found us." Logan reached out to take Jessica's hand, giving it a gentle squeeze. They were totally in sync on this. "We'll pick up some burners. We'll let you know those numbers once we have them."

After a brief hesitation, Wayne nodded. "Okay."

"I would like to know when you and the feds plan to head back up to the mountain." When Jess rose to her feet, Teddy jumped up too. "We'll need to go with you, or you'll never find the place. And

Teddy is your best chance at finding Benton and the drugs."

"I'll let FBI agent Griff Flannery know." Wayne stood. "And as soon as I have your contact information, I'll pass that along to him."

"We'll need a ride to a new location. And it would be nice if you'd stop at a store along the way so we can get those phones." Logan tried to remember what places, if any, they'd passed on the way to the Elk Lodge.

"And don't forget to send someone to get our stuff from the Lodge too," Jessica added. Then she frowned. "We also need one of the officers to drive Shane's SUV to our new location as well."

"What if the gunman recognizes the SUV?" Logan asked.

"I need the supplies from the back for Teddy." She grimaced, then added, "I guess I can ask the officer to bring that stuff to us, while leaving the SUV behind. It makes me nervous, though, not to have a K9 SUV at our disposal."

He turned toward Wayne. "Can your guys do that?"

Wayne didn't look thrilled with their list of requests, but he didn't balk. Logan knew that was likely because nobody, especially the local police, wanted to get on the bad side of the Sullivan family.

Not when they'd done so much for the community.

"Wait here a minute." Wayne gestured to an empty desk. "I need to follow up with my officers and make the arrangements."

He gestured for Jess to take the chair. "Where do you think we should go next?"

"I've been thinking about that." She stared down at Teddy. "I feel bad Chase paid for a suite we can't even use. But I think it would be better to keep him out of this for now."

He frowned. "I don't think your brother will appreciate being out of the loop."

"I know, but he'll just feel like he has to come back here to babysit me, rather than sticking close to his wife and son." She shook her head. "This isn't his problem, it's ours. Let's wait until we're settled and have our new phones. I'll have to give him the new number. He'll go nuts if I don't answer his calls."

That made him feel slightly better. "Okay. I have the cash Benton paid me. We can use that for the room."

"I can't deny I like the idea of using his money to hide from him." Her smile faded. "But my family will reimburse you, Logan. For this and the damage to your plane."

"It's fine." He shrugged off the offer. "I feel like

this is my fault anyway. And like you said, there's some satisfaction in using his own cash against him."

Sergeant Wayne Carter returned a few minutes later. "Okay, who has the keys to the SUV?"

Jess pulled them from her pocket and handed them to him.

"Burt Jones will pick up the supplies from your hotel room and the SUV. Where do you want to go after we pick up the phones?"

"The Great Frontier should have rooms available." Logan knew the place was more reasonably priced as compared to the Elk Lodge.

"I'll let him know on the way." Wayne gestured toward the door. "Let's go."

The ride to the store to pick up disposable phones didn't take long. Logan went inside to grab them, returning ten minutes later. A few people stared in surprise as he slid into the squad, but he ignored them.

"Did you hear if anyone saw the shooter?" He glanced at Wayne as he left the parking lot. "I assume the officers who stayed behind asked around."

"They're still working on that," Wayne said. "People around here generally cooperate. If someone saw the gunman, they'll call and provide the information."

Logan didn't argue. Normally, big crimes like

murder and shootouts didn't happen in small-town Cody or Greybull. And the residents would absolutely band together against outsiders trying to take over.

Which might be why Benton and whoever he was working with had set up a place in the mountains to use as a home base. He also wondered if the items he'd assumed were hunting and fishing gear were really the chemical components needed to make synthetic drugs.

Upon reaching the Great Frontier, he saw another squad waiting in the parking lot. Two squads, both outside a hotel, were much like a neon sign screaming *Look here, look here* to anyone paying attention.

"Hold on, I've changed my mind." Logan twisted in his seat to address Jessica. "This is too obvious. Let's load up our gear and head off on foot."

She took one glance at the hotel and nodded. "Okay, but I'm not staying at the Wild Bill."

"I promise we won't go there." The Wild Bill was known to rent rooms by the hour. Granted, the local police had cracked down on the illegal stuff going on there, but he had no interest in staying in a place like that.

"Hold on. Why the sudden change in plan?" Wayne demanded. "You don't think this place is safe?"

"I'm saying two squads outside one hotel is too many." He pushed open his door. "Thanks for the ride, though."

Wayne muttered something under his breath, got out and opened the back door for Jess and Teddy. The dog stretched, then looked around and sniffed with interest. Reminding himself that Teddy would alert them if the gunman was nearby, he headed over to the second squad to grab their stuff.

It didn't take too long to repack their backpacks. He felt bad for handing Jess her extra-heavy pack, but he hoped it would be fine for a walk through town.

"Don't forget to stay in touch," Wayne called as they headed out.

Logan nodded. With the two squads still parked out front, he headed along the side of the hotel until they were in the back. Then they cut through the opening leading to the next block. It wasn't easy to blend in while carrying large packs with Teddy trotting between them, but he figured this was better than being in a police car.

They walked in silence for long moments, taking every shortcut possible through gas station and store parking lots.

He turned to make sure no one was following. After a solid twenty minutes of walking, they reached a place called the Lumberjack Inn. They had come upon the place from the back of the building.

"How about here?" He eyed Jess. "Not fancy, but better than the Wild Bill."

"I like it." Jess smiled wearily. "And I'll be glad to be done hiking for a while."

"I know." He stared down at her for a long moment, gripped by the insane urge to kiss her. As if reading his mind, she stepped toward him, her blue gaze locked on his. Time seemed to hold still.

Without taking the time to think it through, he pulled her close and kissed her.

8

———————

Logan's kiss was better than she'd expected. It had been a long time since she'd been held in a man's arms. Maybe too long. She hadn't made time to date or have any sort of personal life since her parents' death. And even then, she wouldn't have chosen Logan based on their history.

Now she was second-guessing her decision. Their kiss ended far too quickly when Teddy pressed his body between them to break them apart. She shot her dog an exasperated glance, unsure if she should be glad the dog had brought her back to her senses or upset with him for butting in.

"I, uh, sorry." Logan looked adorably flustered. "I shouldn't have taken advantage of the situation."

"You didn't." Well, he sort of had, but she could

have stopped him. In truth, she'd wanted to kiss him. Their relationship had changed over the past twenty-four hours. From friends to something more. Something she didn't care to name. "I'm sorry about Teddy."

"He's protective of you." Logan patted her K9 on the head. "And that's a good thing."

Normally, she'd agree. But the entire interaction had knocked her off balance. She glanced around, realizing they were still standing outside the back of the Lumberjack Inn. She suddenly remembered how Doug Bridges had nearly been shot in this same spot back in January. The thought made her shiver. "Let's get inside."

"Yeah." He turned to move across the parking lot toward the front of the hotel.

Minutes later, they were inside the spacious lobby. There was a rustic fireplace that emanated warmth. She stayed close to Logan as they approached the front desk. The clerk was a younger woman who eyed them warily. "May I help you?"

"We need a room with two beds," Logan said. "And I need to pay cash since I lost my credit card."

The clerk's gaze darted from Logan to her. Jess managed a smile. "I don't have a credit card either, sorry. But I promise we won't cause any damage."

"I don't think I'm allowed to accept cash." The clerk gnawed on her lower lip. Then she consulted her computer. After a long moment, she looked up. "I can only take cash if you provide an extra hundred dollars as a deposit against damage."

"That's no problem." Logan pulled the cash from his pocket. "Thanks for doing this."

The woman asked for their names. Before Logan could say anything, she spoke up. "I'm Claire Martinson, and this is my husband, Dan."

Logan's face flushed when she alleged they were married, but he didn't say anything to correct her. He simply passed a portion of the cash Craig Benton had given him across the desk.

"Thank you." The clerk took the money and handed over two room keys. "You're in room 126."

"Thanks," Logan said, avoiding the clerk's gaze. Jess hid a smile as she followed him down the hall toward their room.

"This is nice." She glanced around the room with the rustic western motif.

"I was afraid to ask how much a suite would cost." Logan shrugged out of his backpack, dropping it onto the floor near the bed farthest from the bathroom. "Besides, I thought that would be suspicious considering we claimed to have lost our credit cards."

"We'll be fine." Oddly, much like the suite, this room also seemed more intimate than sharing the tent. She dropped her backpack down with a sense of relief. Then she took off her coat and hat. She ran her fingers through her long blond hair, wishing again that she had toiletries to take a shower. "I'll need to call Chase soon. Knowing the grapevine around here, he may have heard about the shooting incident at the park."

Logan removed his winter gear, then bent to pull their new phones from his pack. "Okay. It won't take too long to get these ready to go."

She sat on the edge of the bed, watching as Teddy sniffed the room with interest. He spent so much time sniffing the table between the two beds that she feared he'd alert on the scent of drugs. But he soon lost interest and returned to stretch out at her feet.

"Good boy." She stroked his fur as Logan worked on the phones. "You did a good job today."

Teddy's tail thumped against the carpet.

"Okay, these are being charged up now." Logan sat on the edge of the bed. "Your brother is not going to be happy that we were found at the Elk Lodge."

"True." She sighed. "I don't know how we could have anticipated Benton had the ability to track our phones."

"I've been thinking about that." Logan turned on the edge of the bed to face her. "Whatever Benton is doing up on the mountain must be something big.

A massive drug operation of some sort to justify these attempts to find and kill us."

She nodded slowly. "You're probably right. This can't be just a simple drug handoff between willing participants. They're doing something up on that mountain that they don't want anyone to know about."

"Exactly." Logan scrubbed his hands over his bearded chin. "The more I consider the options, the less I like the idea of you and Teddy being involved in searching for Benton or his drugs."

"There's no other way to find them." Deep down, she wasn't thrilled with the idea of putting her dog in harm's way either. "I can't imagine the site will be easy to find without Teddy's keen nose."

"We have no idea how many people are involved in this." Logan scowled. "Benton, sure, but there could easily be several others."

It was hard to argue his point. She gestured to the phones. "Is there enough of a charge for a quick call?"

He arched a brow. "You really think calling your brother will be quick? He's going to grill you for information."

"He will, but it's not like we know very much. Other than the guy used nine-millimeter ammo." She truly wasn't looking forward to the conversation with Chase and was anxious to get it over with.

"Okay, here." He pulled one phone off the charger. "It's halfway charged."

"Thanks." She punched in Chase's number. Good thing Chase had insisted they memorize each other's numbers. On search and rescue missions, they often had to borrow satellite phones to get through to the rest of the team. And there was no way to preprogram them with their individual numbers. No surprise her call from a strange number went straight to her brother's voice mail. She left a brief message. "Chase, this is Jess, using a different phone. We're fine, not hurt, but there was another incident of gunfire, so we had to go on the move. And get new phones. Call me when you can at this number. Thanks."

Logan winced. "He's going to freak when he hears that."

"I told him we were fine." She stared at the device in her hand. Less than ten seconds later, the phone rang. "Hi, Chase."

"What happened?" her brother demanded.

She quickly filled him in on the recent event. "We're fine. Teddy alerted us to the danger in time. Then he also found the nine-millimeter shell casing. We moved to a new location and ditched our phones as an extra precaution."

"This isn't good, Jess," Chase said somberly. "I

don't like leaving you and Logan hanging in the wind."

"We walked here cutting through streets to stay off the main roads and used cash for the room. That reminds me. Please let Shane know his SUV is at the Elk Lodge."

"The SUV is the least of our worries. And that could be how you were found at the hotel." Chase's tone was grim. "The shooter at Logan's place may have used his rifle scope to get the license plate."

"That's possible. Or he tracked our phones. Benton called Logan's phone to arrange for the charter." She hesitated, then added, "Logan and I think there must be a fairly big drug operation going on to justify these attacks."

"Doug and Maya will be home soon. After their original flight was delayed, they caught a red-eye from the Big Island in Hawaii last night."

She sighed. "I hope they didn't choose the red-eye because of me."

"Maya probably insisted. You know how stubborn she can be."

She rolled her eyes. "We're all stubborn, Chase. It's a Sullivan family trait."

"Yup. So you know there was nothing I could do to convince them to wait for the next daytime flight. The fact is, Doug will be able to reach out to his

DEA colleagues when he gets here. And from there, we can determine our next steps."

"Sounds good." She gave Logan a reassuring smile. "Ask Doug to call me when he's home."

"Will do. Is Logan there?" Chase asked.

"You know he is. Hang on." She held out the phone. Logan took it.

"Hey, Chase." Logan listened intently to whatever Chase was saying for a long minute. "There's no need for that, but thanks for the offer. Don't worry. I think we're safe here. And yes, I'll protect her and so will Teddy. We'll be in touch." He ended the call, then plugged the phone back into the charger. "Your brother is worried about you."

"He takes his role as the head of the household seriously." She shrugged. "Maya does too. To their credit, they held the family together after we lost our parents. Mostly for Kendra's sake." Thinking of her parents only reminded her of the tail piece they'd been forced to leave behind with Logan's plane.

When this was over, she wanted to get the tail fin examined by an expert. If it was a part of their parents' plane, she'd head back up to the mountain to search for the rest of the debris.

It was well past time to get some answers as to what happened that fateful day five and a half years ago.

LOGAN HADN'T NEEDED Chase's warning to take care of Jessica. That was something he'd do regardless. However, the conversation with Chase was a stern reminder that kissing her again was off-limits.

Now and during the foreseeable future.

Just because he'd wanted to kiss her since they were in high school didn't mean he should have acted on the impulse. Especially considering how they'd been standing outside the hotel where the shooter could have easily made another attempt to kill them.

Could he be more of an idiot? He needed to keep his head screwed on straight. Jessica was in danger because of him. He couldn't afford to be distracted by his tangled-up-in-knots feelings for her.

Feelings he'd have sworn weren't returned in kind—until the moment she'd kissed him back. Her embrace had nearly knocked him off his feet.

And made him long for more.

Enough. He gave himself a mental shake, knowing he needed to stay focused on keeping Jessica safe as promised. Logan stood and moved to the window. He peered through the narrow opening between the sheer drapes. Their room overlooked the back of the hotel, which was the way they'd come in, cutting through the parking lot of the pharmacy. He scanned the parking lot, then pulled the darker shades together to keep anyone from seeing inside their room. The resulting dimness made him turn on the desk lamp.

He turned to look at Jess. Chase had assured him that he'd be reimbursed for the room, not that he'd been worried about that. He remembered the bit of conversation he'd overheard between Jess and her brother. "What was that about Doug and Maya?"

"Oh yeah. Their original flight was canceled, so they jumped on a red-eye to get home quicker. They'll back at the ranch sometime today." She frowned. "Doug is going to reach out to his DEA contacts to see if they know anything about Benton or drugs being in the Bighorn Mountains."

"It would be nice if Benton was a known alias." He doubted it would be so easy to find the guy. "I can't imagine why on earth Benton had decided to start up a drug operation in the mountains either. It's not easy to get in and out of the place except by flying or hiking. You'd think they'd want to be somewhere closer to the action."

"Maybe it's a staging area," Jess suggested.

"Could be." He had to admit that someone needed to get back up on that mountain and soon. *Anyone other than Jess*, he thought wearily. He rubbed the stubble on his chin. "I'm going to walk to the pharmacy to pick up a few things, like a razor. Do you want anything?"

"Yes. I'm dying to take a shower." She shot to her feet. "I'll go with you."

He hesitated, then realized she may need personal items, too, and decided not to argue. "Okay. Let's go, then."

"We might want to pick up something to eat." She gestured to the microwave. "It's not a suite, but at least we can heat up something for lunch."

"Okay." He reached for his coat, trying not to think about the long afternoon stretching before them. As strange as it sounded, he'd rather be outside camping in the snow than cooped up in a hotel room with Jess.

Even Teddy wasn't enough of a distraction.

"Hold on." He quickly bent and grabbed their partially charged phones. They weren't going far, but he didn't want to be caught off guard again. "Let's take these with us."

They hadn't even reached the door when one of the phones rang. Knowing the only person so far who had their number was Jess's family, he quickly answered it. "Hello?"

"Logan? It's Chase. Sergeant Wayne Carter is looking for you."

"Why?" He grimaced at the way his tone

sounded suspicious. "I mean, we already told him everything we know."

"For one thing, he claims you promised to provide your new number. The other issue is that he has a few more questions."

Jessica whispered, "What's going on?"

He held up his hand. "Okay, we'll call him. But I don't want anyone to know where we're staying. So if he has more questions, we'll need to meet in a neutral location."

"I'm sure that won't be a problem," Chase said. "I understand your desire to stay off-grid. I didn't even ask Jess where you were staying."

"It's fine if you know we're at the Lumberjack Inn." Logan glanced at his watch. "I'll call Wayne and agree to meet with him in an hour or so." He flashed Jess a reassuring smile. "He can spring for lunch."

"Don't forget, we'll reimburse you for all expenses," Chase said. "I don't care what it takes to keep Jess safe."

"I know. It's fine. Thanks for the update." He ended the call. "Let's head over to the pharmacy. I'll call Wayne once we return."

"I wonder why he wants to talk to us so soon," Jess said as they headed outside. Teddy trotted between them, his head up and ears pricked forward. "It's barely been a half hour since we left him."

"I have no idea." Although Logan was afraid that whatever had come up wasn't good news.

Thankfully, they didn't see a single person as they cut across the rear parking lot to the drugstore. He grabbed what he needed, then waited at the register for Jessica. Even though they'd each only gotten the essentials, the bill was still higher than he'd expected.

He hid a wince. At this rate, he'd be out of cash before the end of the day.

They hurried back to the Lumberjack Inn. "You go first," he said. "I'll call Wayne."

"Thanks." Jess carried her bag of toiletries into the bathroom. Left behind, Teddy heaved a sigh as he stretched out in front of the bathroom door.

Wayne answered on the first ring. "Sergeant Carter."

"It's Logan. You may want to make a note of this number."

"It's about time you called," Wayne groused. "Where are you?"

"Our location doesn't matter. Chase mentioned you wanted to talk. Why? Has something happened?"

"I do want to talk to you and Jessica," Wayne said without answering his question. "Tell me where you are and I'll send someone to pick you up."

He frowned, wondering what could have happened to cause this sudden request. "How about we meet you for lunch, say in an hour?"

"Lunch?" Wayne repeated.

"Yeah, you know, the midday meal? We're hungry. And if you want to interview us again in person, you'll need to meet us at the Hitching Post. We'll walk there rather than ride in a squad."

There was a long pause, as if Wayne was facing a monumental decision.

"Look, if you don't want to meet in person, we can talk over the phone," Logan said. "I'd like to understand what's going on. I can put the call on speaker so Jessica can be a part of the conversation."

"I'd rather meet in person," Wayne said. "I'll meet you and Jessica at the Post in an hour."

"See you then." Logan lowered the phone with a feeling of unease. If he didn't know better, he'd think Wayne was suddenly treating them like suspects.

Rather than victims of multiple attempts to kill them.

What could have changed? He stood and found the TV remote. Turning it on, he found a news station.

The TV anchors were discussing the upcoming Easter holiday. He had to increase the volume a bit when Jess turned on the blow-dryer.

He was disappointed there weren't any breaking news stories.

"Your turn," Jess announced as she emerged from the bathroom. She eyed the TV curiously. "What's up?"

"Nothing new from what I can tell." He left the TV on and reached for his bag of toiletries. "We're meeting with Wayne at the Post for lunch. He didn't fill me in about why he was so anxious to have another in-person interview, so I was hoping to catch something on the news."

She stepped over Teddy, who finally scrambled to his feet, and came over to join him. "That's odd."

"Yeah. Maybe you should keep watching for a while."

"I will." She dropped down on the edge of the bed. "Here, Teddy."

The dog once again stretched out beside her. Logan brushed past them to head into the bathroom. The enticing scent of Jessica's shampoo teased his senses, but he reminded himself to stay focused.

He made quick work of his shower and shave. He wished he had clean clothes to change into, but that was a luxury he couldn't afford to spend cash on.

Old clothes would have to do. Even if they

smelled like smoke from their campfire the night before.

A scent he'd now associate with Jessica, he thought wryly.

He opened the bathroom door and nearly tripped over Teddy. He was surprised to see the dog outside the door. "I thought he was protecting you."

"He was. Then he decided to protect you." She gestured to the TV. "Sorry to say there's been nothing exciting in the news."

"Maybe the police are keeping whatever happened under wraps," he said. "Not easy to do in a small town full of gossips."

"More likely we're overreacting to Wayne's request for a meeting." Jess stood. "I think we should leave now. Better to get there well before the cops arrive."

She had a point about both the overreacting and getting to the Hitching Post early. Although his nerves were still on edge over the upcoming meeting. He forced a smile. "Okay, let's go. And we'll plan on taking the back roads again."

"That works for me." She shrugged into her coat, glancing down at her K9. "Poor Teddy just wants to rest, and we keep dragging him around town."

He didn't think the dog looked too tired. Logan drew on his coat and then disconnected the phones, handing one to her. She turned the TV off, then reached for the door.

Retracing their earlier steps, they crossed the parking lot to the drugstore. From there, they cut through another street, before making a large loop around town to reach the Hitching Post.

There was no sign of a squad out front when they approached. The bad news was that Jessica and Teddy tended to attract attention. Several customers smiled when they saw the dog, who tended to look happy when he wasn't barking.

The Post was a seat-yourself kind of place. He hadn't been there in years, but he was glad to see it hadn't changed much. Spying a booth in the back, he quickly headed toward it. Jessica and Teddy followed. Teddy immediately stretched out on the floor beneath the table and went to sleep.

Maybe he was tired.

A moment later, a harried-looking server approached. "What would ya like to drink?"

"Coffee," he and Jess answered simultaneously.

When she'd filled their mugs, they placed their lunch orders, then sipped their coffee in silence. Five minutes before the designated meeting time, Sergeant Wayne Carter strode into the café. He stood looking around for a moment before spotting them.

"Thanks for coming," Wayne said in a brisk tone.

Logan was tempted to point out that they didn't have much of a choice but held his tongue as the cop settled into the booth beside him. Wayne asked for coffee too. It didn't take long for him to get straight to the point.

"You didn't mention the fact that your girlfriend died of a drug overdose." Wayne's gaze bored into Logan's.

"Why would I? That was eight years ago." He didn't bother to hide his annoyance. "That has nothing to do with what's going on now."

"I'm not so sure about that," Wayne drawled. "Tell me again why you assumed this Benton guy had drugs on the plane?"

"Teddy alerted," Jessica said. "He's trained to alert on the scent of drugs."

"Yeah, but you said yourself he's been cross-trained to scent other items," Wayne pointed out. "He found the shell casing."

Jess flushed and glanced at Logan. "Yes, but that's because I told him to search for gold. That's the term we use for gun powder and gun oil."

"Okay, but it seems to me the dog could have alerted on the scent of a gun in the plane," Wayne said.

"I guess that's possible," Jess admitted. "Based

on the glove that he found, it could be that Benton held a gun while wearing it. Or had the gun in his pocket with the glove."

Logan didn't like where this was going. "Are you saying you don't think this is about drugs?"

"Oh, I absolutely think this is about drugs," Wayne said. "I just wanted to understand why you jumped on the drug bandwagon. Then I heard from the chief about how Ella Dover had died of a drug overdose while dating you, Logan."

He wondered if he'd ever be able to shake off his connection to Ella's death. "I had nothing to do with that. I didn't even know she was on drugs."

"I didn't know that either, and I was her friend," Jessica added.

"So it would surprise both of you to learn her brother, Ethan, died of a drug overdose earlier today?" Wayne asked.

Logan's jaw dropped. He turned to stare at Jessica who looked just as horrified by the news.

Ethan Dover overdosed on drugs? What did that mean? Had Ethan been involved in drugs back when his sister overdosed?

Or was this something that he'd recently gotten tangled up in?

Either way, it was clear that Ethan's death was part of whatever was going on now.

9

————

Ethan was dead from a drug overdose? Jessica couldn't imagine the guy she'd known doing something like this. Ethan had been so upset over Ella's death, railing at his sister's use of drugs.

Maybe Jess was being naïve, but she couldn't believe Ethan had gone down that same path. Not the Ethan she'd known. "There's no way Ethan used drugs."

Wayne arched a brow. "I can assure you he died of an overdose."

"Okay, so maybe that's true, but I'm telling you he wasn't a user." She narrowed her eyes at the cop. "Maybe someone used drugs to kill him specifically to make it look like an overdose."

"And why would anyone do that?" Wayne did

not shy away from her gaze. "Did Ethan have any enemies that you're aware of?"

"No." She glanced at Logan, who looked thoughtful. "I just think it's too much of a coincidence. We're looking for a guy who may have transported drugs on Logan's plane, followed by several attempts to kill us, then suddenly Ethan Dover is found dead of a drug overdose." A thought occurred to her. "What sort of drugs? Fentanyl?"

"Yes," Wayne acknowledged. "Fentanyl. Same as his sister."

No one spoke for a long minute. Their server brought their food, then asked Wayne what he wanted. He ordered a burger.

Jessica gave a silent prayer before taking a bite of her chicken sandwich. Logan's cheeseburger looked good too.

"I agree with Jess," Logan said between bites. "Something's not right."

Wayne sat back in his seat. "It's interesting that you both had connections to the Dover siblings."

"Most of our classmates knew the Dover siblings." Logan waved a hand toward the window and the people milling about outside. "This town isn't that big. Everyone knows everyone else around here."

Another long silence. She had the impression Wayne was waiting for them to fill in additional details, which was ridiculous because they didn't know anything.

At least, she didn't. She shot another quick look at Logan.

"Tell me about those classmates of yours." Wayne pulled a small notebook from his pocket. "Start with those closest to the Dover siblings."

"Ella, Julie Plumber, Cindy Deets, and I were all relatively close," Jessica said when Logan didn't immediately respond. "I knew Ethan because he was in Chase's class." She winced, belatedly realizing she'd added another connection between the Sullivans and the Dovers.

"Go on," Wayne said when she fell silent.

She swallowed hard. It was too late to go back. And as Logan said, everyone knew everyone else here. "Ethan was also friends with Julie's older brother, Greg Plumber." She tried to think about who else to include. "I believe Matt Salvatore was another friend of theirs. To be honest, I've lost touch with many of my former classmates. First, I moved away to work in Cheyenne, then more recently as we've started taking on more and more search and rescue missions." She figured it wouldn't hurt to reinforce the good things her family had done for the community, especially over these past five years. "Living on the ranch can be isolating."

"What about you?" Wayne shifted to look at Logan.

"Greg served time in the army," Logan said. "I didn't know Matt very well. But Ella dated Andy Tolliver before me."

"Andy was another friend of ours. He was super smart; he got a full ride to Montana State University." Jess smiled at the memory. Andy was deemed the most successful of their senior class. "But like the others, I don't know where he is now."

Wayne continued scribbling in his notebook. When their server brought his hamburger, he nodded in thanks, tried a french fry, then stared back down at his notebook. "I'm sure I can find out where these kids are now." He looked up. "Any of them involved in drugs? Or were there other kids that were known to use?"

"Sure, there were kids that smoked pot," Logan said. "I don't know of anyone doing major drugs like cocaine, heroin, meth, or fentanyl."

"Me either," Jess agreed. "Could be the potheads did other stuff too, but if so, they kept it quiet."

"Ella would have had to get drugs from someone," Wayne pointed out. He pushed his notebook aside to take a bite of his burger.

"The cops asked me about that back when she died." Logan's tone had a hard edge to it. "I told them the same thing I'm telling you now. Ella may have gone to the potheads for information related to buying drugs. That seems the most logical avenue. But I have no knowledge of that. She never used drugs with me. And I never saw her impaired from drugs." He grimaced, and added, "I did see her drinking one night at a party. But that was the extent of the illegal activity I was aware of."

"What party?" Jess stared at Logan. "I don't know anything about that."

"It was after one of the football games." He shifted in his seat and sighed. "We argued that night. I wanted to leave; she didn't. I felt obligated to stay to make sure she got home safely."

"Which game?" She was trying to figure out why she hadn't been there. Then she remembered. "It must have been the one I missed because of my sprained my knee. I remember having to sit home all weekend alternating ice and heat."

"Yep." Logan nodded. "I remember you weren't around. That guy you used to date, Jerrod, was at the party, though. He seemed to be quite cozy with Nina Jenson."

She shrugged. "Jerrod was free to cozy up to whomever he wanted. Didn't matter to me. We were broken up by then." She frowned, then added, "I remember that my knee was still sore at Ella's funeral, so the party must have been what, two weeks before her death?"

"Yes, about that," Logan agreed. "Which is exactly what I told the police back then."

"I reviewed the police reports, and I was struck by the way you mentioned that you only saw Ella drinking that one time at the party. Not at any other after-school event." Wayne eyed them skeptically. "Give me a break. I know high school kids, and I am convinced there must have been other parties where kids were drinking."

"Oh, there were plenty of parties," Jess said with a nod. "And sure, there were lots of kids who drank and smoked pot. But I wasn't one of them. I didn't like to get drunk."

"And why was that?" Wayne asked.

"For me, it was a control thing." She glanced at Logan. "I seem to remember you didn't do much partying either."

"You're right, I didn't." Logan shrugged. "To be honest, the one time I got drunk, I was so sick the next day I thought I was going to die. Avoiding alcohol was easy after that. Just smelling it made me nauseous. And I never liked the smell of pot either. Since my goal was to fly planes, I told everyone I had to stay sober to keep my pilot's license." He offered a wry smile. "I preferred taking on the role of designated driver."

Jess hadn't known about his hangover, but it made sense.

"Lots of kids drink or do drugs to release their inhibitions." Wayne looked from her to Logan and back. "It stands to reason that could be why Ella sought out some drugs after that night of partying."

Logan sighed and shook his head. "That's not the Ella I remember."

She understood his frustration. Anything was possible, but speculating wasn't helpful. She turned her attention to Wayne. "From what Ethan told me, Ella didn't have the physical signs of long-term drug use."

"I know she didn't have needle marks or anything like that," Logan said. "Not while we were together."

"That's true. I read her autopsy report," Wayne agreed. "No needle marks or other physical evidence to indicate she used drugs. And to be honest, her brother's death is very similar in that way, at least from what I can tell. We'll have to wait on the autopsy results to know that for sure."

"Are you suggesting they were murdered?" Logan's expression was shocked.

"No." Wayne shook his head and munched another fry. "There's no evidence they were drugged against their will. Especially in Ella's case, as she was at home when she overdosed. But it could be that their one and only attempt to get high resulted in the overdose that led to their deaths. Fentanyl is a hundred times stronger than heroin or meth. The reason these drug dealers are mixing fentanyl with other drugs to primarily to get people hooked so they buy more and more." Wayne shook his head and sighed. "My theory at this point is that Ella and Ethan must have tried some pot laced with fentanyl. If the drug dealer was high himself, he may not have realized the impact fentanyl could have on someone who was a first-time user."

"So you think this was an accidental overdose, then," Logan said grimly. "Because a drug dealer would know that dead drug addicts don't continue to buy product."

"Exactly," Wayne agreed.

"No way. I just can't see Ethan doing that." She couldn't say the same about Ella. During the time her friend had been seeing Logan, their friendship had been a bit strained. She'd always thought it was strange that Ella had died at home in her own bed. "He would never touch drugs after the way he lost his sister."

"Eight years is a long time. Ethan may have changed his mind on that front." Wayne finished his burger, then tucked his notebook back in his breast pocket. "Thanks for meeting with me to go over these things. I appreciate your insight."

To Jess's mind, this had been more of an interrogation than a conversation. She and Logan had clearly been in the hot seat, forced to prove their innocence. Her appetite had faded as they'd talked.

Drugs and death.

And murder?

Wayne pulled cash from his pocket and dropped it on the table. Then he rose to his feet. His movement startled Teddy, making him scramble out from beneath the table.

"Thanks for lunch," Logan said as the cop turned away.

"Yes, thank you." She turned to Teddy. "Lie down. We'll be leaving soon."

"What do you make of that?" Logan gestured toward Wayne's retreating figure. "He acted as if we were keeping secrets from him or something."

"I know. Especially since he could have gotten those names of our respective classmates from the police reports that were submitted back when Ella died." She forced herself to finish her meal since she had no idea when they'd get a chance to eat again. "I know they interviewed everyone who was close to Ella."

"Tell me about it," Logan muttered. "I was their prime suspect for a long time. In fact, Ethan accused me of helping Ella get the drugs."

She winced and nodded. "I know."

"There's something fishy about his death," Logan continued. "I find it hard to believe he just up and decided to try drugs. Especially something like fentanyl."

She leaned forward, propping her elbows on the table. "Do you think Ethan was digging into something drug related and was killed to shut him up?"

"It sounds kinda crazy when you say it out loud." He finished his burger and pushed his empty plate away. "But yeah, I do."

She thought about that for a long moment. "Wouldn't Ethan go to the police if he suspected drugs were being made or sold here in Cody?"

"Maybe he was looking for proof before going to the cops." Logan frowned. "What was Ethan doing for work these days?"

"He works, or rather, *worked* for the general store. I saw him there a couple of weeks ago." She abruptly stood. Teddy also scrambled to his feet as if ready to go. "Stay, Teddy." Then to Logan, she added, "I need to use the restroom. When I'm finished, we should head over to the general store."

"Why would we do that?" Logan frowned. "I doubt we'll learn anything, as the police likely already questioned Ethan's coworkers. Besides that, we're supposed to be staying off-grid."

He was right on both counts. Yet hearing about Ethan's death bothered her. She totally agreed there was something off about his alleged drug overdose. "I don't care. We're here and the store is only a few blocks away. We can make a quick stop there before returning to the hotel."

Logan stood. "I need to take a quick break, too, so take Teddy with you. I'll meet you at the front door."

"Sounds good. Come, Teddy." She led the way to the restrooms, where they went their separate ways. She and Teddy waited near the front door for Logan. She eyed the street, hoping the gunman wasn't lurking nearby.

There was no sign of Wayne or any other cops patrolling the streets. The Cody police department was small, and she knew full well there were only four cops on duty during the daytime. Two officers covered the night shift and weekends. The group of officers rotated between the day and night shifts, alternating every third weekend. They had some help from the state police who patrolled the highways. This wasn't exactly a high crime area, which made her realize the four officers on duty were likely still dealing with Ethan's death.

She wished she'd thought to ask Wayne where Ethan's body was found.

At work? At home? Someplace else?

It made her wonder if their small police presence was the reason Benton had chosen this location for their illegal drug trade. It seemed counterintuitive, as small towns were far more aware of outsiders. It would be easier to get lost in the crowd of a big city.

But at times like this, one major crime scene could suck up the police resources, leaving the rest of the city vulnerable. Accidental or murder? It was troubling that Ethan had died so young.

And his passing made it all the more imperative that they find Benton and soon. Before anyone else suffered the same fate.

LOGAN JOINED Jess and Teddy at the main entrance to the restaurant. He didn't like the plan of heading to the general store. "Let's just go back to the hotel."

"We practically have to walk by the store to get there." She shot him a questioning glance. "What can it hurt?"

"If you ask me, there would be more information to be gained from checking out Ethan's home than stopping by the store." He swept his gaze over the area, then turned and led the way to the back of the restaurant to avoid the main street through town.

"He lived in his parents' old house." Jess grimaced. "They moved down to Arizona after Ella's death."

"If I remember correctly, that's not far from

here." He eyed Teddy, knowing the dog was the best early alert system they had. "Are you up for a walk?"

"Why not?" She grinned. "Piece of cake considering how far we hiked yesterday and earlier today."

"I'm sure the police have already searched the place, but I wouldn't mind checking it out." He fell in behind her.

Jess eagerly set out, with Teddy trotting alongside. She threw an arched glance at him over her shoulder. "Better than sitting and staring at each other in the hotel room."

He flushed, silently admitting that was exactly why he'd suggested this detour. Which was ridiculous as they both deserved some downtime.

Yet here they were, heading to the home of his dead girlfriend and her now also deceased brother.

They walked in silence, taking several shortcuts the same way they had earlier. Thankfully, nobody seemed to notice.

When they reached the small neighborhood to the north, Jess stayed on the street. Teddy sniffed and occasionally lifted his leg to mark his territory.

The Dover home was on Baker Street, the second house from the corner. Seeing it after all these years was a bit of a shock. For some reason, the white cape cod–style home looked much smaller than he remembered.

"I don't see a police officer," Jess said in a low voice. "That's odd, isn't it?"

He nodded. "I expected there to be someone here. Makes me think Ethan's body was found someplace else."

"We should have asked Wayne about that." Jess stood at the end of the driveway. "It looks more run-down than I remember."

"Yeah. Doesn't look like Ethan put much money into upkeep. At least, not on the exterior. Could be he spent his money on the inside."

Jess glanced around, then started up the drive-way. "Let's look through the window."

They had no business being there, but he followed her and Teddy up the driveway to the front of the small home. When Jess headed to a window, he followed. Teddy sniffed along the ground without alerting.

He took that as a good sign.

The window revealed a living room that looked exactly the way he remembered. Whatever Ethan was spending his money on, it wasn't remodeling the house. It was creepy that Ethan had chosen to stay and live there without doing anything to change the place, knowing his sister had died in her room.

"Nothing has changed," Jessica whispered.

"Nope." He stepped back. "Let's get out of here.

It's only a matter of time until the cops show up. Wayne will be more suspicious of our motives if he finds us standing here, gawking like this."

"I haven't been here since Ella's passing." Jess stepped back, bumping into Teddy who scrambled out of the way. "I can't imagine why Ethan didn't sell the place so he could start over someplace new."

He thought about how he'd sold his mother's place. He'd felt a little guilty but had known it was for the best. "Maybe we're wrong about Ethan not doing drugs. Living here with the constant memories of Ella's death could have changed him, and not for the better."

"I don't know. He seemed normal when I ran into him a few weeks ago." She turned and stepped up to try the front door. "It's locked."

"Like I said, the cops will likely be here soon." He watched as Teddy sniffed along the base of the door. "Maybe we should call Wayne and offer to use Teddy's nose to see if there are drugs inside?"

Jess's blue eyes widened with interest. "That's a great idea."

He quickly pulled out his phone and found Wayne's number. The sergeant didn't answer, so he left a brief message. "It's Logan. Jess and Teddy would like to help you search Ethan's house for drugs. Call me back."

"Let's start now," Jess suggested. "Teddy can

search the outside while we wait to hear from Wayne."

"Okay." He swept another glance around the neighborhood. It was rather quiet, maybe because it was the middle of the day during the middle of the week when most people were working.

Jess bent over Teddy. "Are you ready to work? Are you?" She injected excitement into her tone. "I need you to search. Search, Teddy. Peppers! Search for peppers!"

Teddy's tail wagged with enthusiasm at the idea of playing the search game. The K9 made a quick circle and began to sniff along the edge of the front yard where patches of snow had melted revealing brown grass. Teddy sniffed long and hard before trotting across the yard toward the side of the house.

He and Jess followed. Logan figured the only way Teddy would alert on drugs outside the home was if a drug dealer had dropped off his product in person.

An unlikely scenario.

Still, he trailed along behind Jess and Teddy, watching with admiration as Teddy worked. The K9 was eager to please, and he wondered how the dog would handle the disappointment of not winning at the game.

Teddy spent a little extra time at the back door, clearly sifting through various scents before moving on. The dog seemed to be following some invisible trail that only he could follow.

When Teddy abruptly veered off toward the detached two-car garage, Logan's pulse kicked up.

If they were wrong about Ethan, and the guy was buying drugs, maybe he had decided to keep them in the garage? He quickened his pace to keep up.

"Search! Search for peppers," Jess called. Although from what Logan could tell, the K9 didn't need extra encouragement. The way Teddy's nose was tracking along the ground, the dog was clearly in work mode.

The dog stopped in front of the garage, sniffing along the bottom of the garage door. He was about to cross over to peer through the service door window when Teddy abruptly lifted his head to look around.

"What is it, boy?" Jess asked.

The dog's ears pricked forward as he sniffed the air. Then he began to growl, his eyes seemingly focused on something to the left of the garage.

The gunman?

"Jess, get down!" Logan reached into his pocket for his gun as he frantically searched the area for a sign of Benton or whomever had caught Teddy's attention. He trusted the dog's instincts over his own. When he didn't see anything alarming, he darted over to where Jessica and Teddy were huddled up against the right side of the garage.

Teddy's low growling grew louder. Then he let out a series of sharp barks. The dog made such a racket he imagined any neighbors that might be home would be looking out their windows to find the source of the annoying noise.

"Where is he?" Jessica asked in a hushed tone.

"I'm not sure." He'd expected to hear gunfire, but there was nothing above Teddy's barking. He didn't like the way they were out in the open. The garage didn't offer that much protection. "Maybe Teddy scared him off."

"I hope so," Jess murmured.

He didn't bother to point out that the dog hadn't stopped the gunman from trying to kill them earlier. Before he could say anything more, the sound of police sirens filled the air. He stayed where he was, intending to protect Jessica and Teddy until he knew for sure the threat was neutralized.

Yet his thoughts whirled. This was another near miss. One of these times, they wouldn't escape unscathed.

Was it possible one of the neighbors had spotted them snooping and had called the police?

If so, the simple act may have saved their lives.

10

———————

Jess huddled next to Logan with Teddy at her side, listening as the police sirens grew louder with the approaching squads. She closed her eyes and silently thanked God for continuing to protect them. If not for His mercy, she felt certain she and Logan would already be dead.

And if they didn't do something different soon, she was afraid the gunman would succeed in taking them out of the equation. Teddy had alerted them to the danger once again.

She and Logan didn't move until the two responding officers, Burt Jones and his rookie Tim Riley, headed toward the garage. Logan straightened and quickly dropped his weapon back into his coat pocket.

"We're fine," he called. "But Teddy alerted us to danger."

"What are you doing here?" Burt glared at her. "I thought you were going to stay off-grid."

"That was the plan." She rested her hand on Teddy's head. "We heard about Ethan Dover's death and thought it might be helpful to have Teddy search for drugs."

Burt scowled. "Did Wayne agree to that?"

"We reached out to him." She glanced at Logan who pulled out his phone, then shook his head. "Not yet. But it stands to reason that if Ethan had overdosed on drugs, there would be some here at his place."

Burt heaved a sigh. "We got a call about someone lurking near the property. When we realized it was Ethan's house, we quickly responded."

"Did the caller report one person or two?" Logan asked. "Because Teddy began to growl and bark shortly before you headed over. We believe he caught the scent of the gunman."

"Two people." Tim, the rookie waved at them. "And a dog. We thought it might be you."

"Too bad, I was hoping for a description of the gunman." Logan scowled.

Burt eyed Teddy, then glanced at his rookie partner. "I've seen the Sullivan K9s in action. If they think the dog alerted on someone, then I believe them. Let's do a sweep of the property to check things out."

Tim looked slightly annoyed but didn't argue. She and Logan waited as the two officers spread out and looked around the exterior of the house and garage.

Logan's phone rang, and from his wry expression, she deduced the caller was Wayne. "This is Fletcher, and yes, I'm here with Jess and Teddy at Ethan's house." He winced and held the phone from his ear. "No need to yell, we just thought it would be helpful to ask Teddy to search for drugs."

No surprise the cops were upset with their interference in their investigation. Yet in their defense, it was Wayne who'd asked for a meeting. And who had informed them of Ethan's death due to a drug overdose.

Not to mention they were the ones being hunted by some unknown gunman.

"Yes, the offer stands. We'll wait here. Thanks." Logan lowered the phone. "Wayne has reluctantly agreed to use Teddy to search the house for drugs. He had to get a search warrant but is on his way."

"Great." She stroked Teddy's fur. "I hope he finds something useful."

"Me too," Logan agreed.

Burt and Tim returned a few minutes later. "I

found a set of footprints in the snow behind the garage. Do you want to take a look?"

"Yes." Logan reached for her hand. "Did you take pictures of them?"

"Of course, but they're not very clear. Looks like the guy came in from the street behind the house, then retraced his footsteps back out again."

"Same way he did at the park, which proves Teddy alerted on the gunman's scent." Jess was concerned about how close they were to being shot. As they rounded the corner of the garage, she noticed the prints stopped about six feet from the garage. Easy to imagine the gunman freezing in place upon hearing Teddy's barking. He must have quickly changed his mind and turned to leave.

"I agree, there aren't any clear prints," Logan said with a frown. "Although the size is approximately a men's eleven."

"Like that will narrow down our perp," Tim said in a snide tone.

For a rookie, he had quite the attitude. Jess held Tim's gaze for a long moment. "I'm sure you realize that the print will be more helpful once you have someone in custody."

The rookie shrugged and looked away. "Whatever."

Logan took pictures as well—why, she wasn't sure—then they all headed back to the front of the house. Teddy hadn't alerted on drugs outside the structures, which left the inside.

And if that was clean, she would lean toward Ethan's death being murder rather than an accidental drug overdose.

Five minutes later, Wayne arrived. He did not look the least bit happy to see her and Logan. He gestured to his officers who crossed over to join him. The three men spoke in low voices for a moment.

"Okay, Jess. We're going to access the house. We'll need you and Logan to stay back until we've cleared the place. I'll let you know when we're ready for Teddy to do his thing."

"Sounds good." She smiled, but Wayne didn't return the sentiment. He used a key that he must have gotten from Ethan's pocket to get inside. Burt and Tim followed him.

"We owe Teddy a big steak for alerting us to the danger," Logan said when they were alone outside the squad.

"No steak, it's not good for him, but maybe a sweet potato treat, hmm?" She bent to pat Teddy's head. "Anna bakes them by the dozen, and the dogs love them." She grinned. "People can eat them too."

"Ah, no thanks. Although they would have come in handy last night." Logan straightened. "Looks like they're ready for us."

Jess glanced over to see Wayne waving them in.

She bent and looked into Teddy's dark-brown eyes. "Are you ready to search? Are you?" When his tail began to wag, she strode forward. "Peppers! Search for peppers!"

Teddy followed her up to the front door of the house, then immediately lowered his nose to the floor as they entered. She focused on her dog, peripherally aware of the messy interior. Ethan was not a neat guy.

She took Teddy through the house one room at a time, offering him encouragement along the way. Ethan's bedroom and bathroom were last. If they were going to find peppers, a.k.a. drugs, this seemed the most logical place.

Teddy did his best. He nosed every nook and cranny of both areas but didn't alert. Jess almost wished she had drugs of some sort so she could reward him.

He gazed up at her, clearly waiting for another command. She knelt and hugged him.

"You did good, Teddy. Really good." She had to laugh when he licked her face. "We'll try again later."

"What about the garage?" Logan suggested.

Wayne shrugged. "We may as well check there. Ethan was in his car when he was found, so the vehicle isn't inside."

Jess headed out the back door with Teddy. Burt

opened the garage for them. Peering in, she noted a push lawn mower, a couple of rakes, and a small workbench. She held Teddy's gaze. "Search! Search for peppers!"

Once again, Teddy lowered his nose and began sniffing along the length of the structure. Then he abruptly turned and zeroed in on the corner of the workbench. He sniffed the drawer there for a long moment, then sat and let out a sharp bark.

His alert! She turned to Burt. "Open it up."

Burt was still wearing the gloves he'd donned upon entering the house. He reached for the drawer and opened it. Jess was close enough to see a bag of what appeared to be pot sitting in the corner.

"Well, well, seems as if Ethan was a user after all," Burt drawled.

Unconvinced, she glanced at Logan. He nodded, acknowledging her thought. "Or they were planted there to add credence to his overdose death."

"Why go to the trouble?" Burt asked.

"To throw us off course." Jess gestured to the baggie in his hands. "I highly recommend the contents of that baggie be closely examined for fentanyl. Touching pure fentanyl powder with your bare hands can be enough to overdose."

Burt eyed the baggie critically, then nodded. "Yeah, we've all been warned about that possibility." He shrugged, then added, "Your dog is amazing."

"Yes, he sure is." She turned to her K9. "Good boy, Teddy!" She crossed over to the open garage door and pulled out his stuffed moose. She tossed it into the air. "Good boy!"

Teddy's body practically vibrated with excitement as he leaped up to grab the toy. Then he ran through the yard, shaking the stuffed moose from side to side. As she watched, she thought about what Wayne had said about Ethan's body being found in his car.

And the drugs were found in an obvious hiding place in his garage. A garage that would be easier to break into without being seen compared to entering someone's house. Interesting how the gunman had approached the property from behind the garage. It could be that it was a trip he'd made before in the not-so-distant past.

She was anxious to talk to her new brother-in-law, Doug Bridges, about what they'd learned today. Having worked many drug cases as a DEA agent, Doug's take on this would be of interest. Because despite the way Teddy had found the baggie, she truly believed this was all an elaborate setup.

A way to hide the fact that Ethan Dover had been brutally murdered.

Too bad they had no idea why the young man had been killed.

LOGAN EYED the baggie in Burt's gloved hand, wondering who'd put it inside the garage. The gunman who Teddy had scared away? Probably. He wasn't buying the theory that Ethan stored his drugs out here.

No drug user would do such a thing. They'd keep their stash close at hand. He'd fully expected Teddy to find the drugs in Ethan's bedside table. The most obvious place for them to be kept.

From the skeptical expression emanating from Jess's gaze, he knew they were of the same mindset. And found himself hoping the local cops were smart enough to see through the ruse.

"I'll ask our crime scene techs to head out here when they've finished processing the vic's car." Wayne nodded at Jess. "Good work finding his stash."

Logan suppressed a sigh. Maybe the local cops weren't as smart as he thought. "Don't you think it's odd the drugs were in the garage?"

Wayne frowned. "You're an expert on drug users?"

"My brother-in-law, Doug Bridges, is a former DEA agent." Jess put a hand on Logan's arm, silently asking him not to argue. "I think it would be a good idea to get his opinion on this. I agree with Logan, though. It seems more logical to me that a drug user would keep their stash close at hand. Not tucked off in the garage."

Wayne hesitated for a long moment. "I wouldn't mind hearing Bridge's thoughts on this. I'll give him a call."

"He should be back at the ranch soon," Logan said. "Last time we spoke with Chase, Doug and Maya were on their way home via a red-eye."

"Fine. We'll run this past him," Wayne agreed. "Thanks for your help, Jess. Teddy too. You may as well head back to the hotel now. We don't need your help from this point forward."

Logan swallowed his annoyance. "One more question, if you don't mind." When Wayne didn't respond, he pushed forward. "Where was Ethan's car found? Here in town or somewhere else?"

"Here in town," Wayne said.

"At the general store?" Jessica guessed.

"Yeah." Wayne scowled. "I guess there's no reason to keep it a secret. Word will have spread across town by now anyway. We had gone there to interview him. The owner mentioned that Ethan was a no call, no show. That's when Burt spotted his car in the back corner of the parking lot."

Logan realized that if they'd have gone to the store, they'd have seen the crime scene tape blocking off the parking lot. Instead, they'd come here and had nearly been caught by the gunman.

"Do you have Ethan's estimated time of death?" Jess asked.

"Sometime after midnight," Wayne admitted. "We'll know more when the doc is finished with the autopsy."

Interesting. Logan wondered if Ethan had been taken to the general store against his will. Or if the gunman had met him there after work. Those details would have to be determined by the cops who would try to retrace Ethan's last movements.

For now, their work was done here. He glanced at Jess. "You ready to go?"

"Yes." She turned to her K9. "Come, Teddy."

The dog had been galivanting around with his stuffed moose, but the moment Jessica called out to him, he trotted to her side and dropped the toy at her feet. She bent to retrieve it.

Logan scanned their surroundings, then gestured toward the back of Ethan's garage. "I say we follow those tracks. See where the gunman may have left his vehicle."

She considered that for a moment before nodding. "Okay. Although I'm sure he's long gone by now."

"I know. But we don't want to take the obvious route back to the hotel." He took a moment to look at the neighboring homes, knowing one of the owners had likely called the police on him and Jess. But it was hard to be upset. He liked knowing that people around here cared about their neighbors.

He cut a parallel path to the footprints in case the crime scene techs could do something with them. Jessica and Teddy were both on high alert, too, as they came out on the other side of the block. The street had been well plowed, so he couldn't tell where the gunman's car may have been parked.

Around here, you couldn't get too far away from Cody without a vehicle. Which only reminded him of the way Benton had requested a charter flight to the mountain. He obviously would have had to meet someone there.

Was the gunman Benton? Or someone else? They had yet to get close enough to figure that out.

"The more run-ins we have with this guy, the more I want to head back up the mountain," Jess said, breaking the silence. "That's where this all started. And I have a feeling that going back will be the only way to end it."

He wished he didn't agree with her. But he felt the same way. "Maybe Shane or one of your brothers could take Teddy up there."

"What?" She spun around to stare at him. "No, Logan. That's not happening. I'm Teddy's handler.

Besides, I can't stay back while putting my siblings in danger."

"Okay, okay." He held his hands up in defeat. "But I'm going on record in saying this is a bad idea."

"Duly noted," she snapped. "You can stay back if you'd like. I'm more than capable of retracing our steps with Doug."

"Oh, I'm going." Logan took a deep breath, fighting the flash of anger. "It was my plane he tried to take down."

"Whatever." She acted as if she couldn't have cared what he did.

Their earlier closeness, including their amazing kiss, seemed like eons ago. And maybe that was for the better. It wasn't as if he didn't admire her skill and dedication. Along with Teddy's incredible nose. His concern was for her safety.

And heading back up to the mountain felt akin to meeting the bear in his den.

They continued walking in silence, darting through side streets to avoid traveling on the main routes. Now that he knew one of Ethan's neighbors had called the police, he tried to choose their shortcuts along properties that appeared deserted.

Their circuitous route added extra time so that it was almost a full twenty minutes before they arrived back at the Lumberjack Inn. Once they were safely inside their room, he and Jessica stripped off their winter gear. Logan ran his hands through his hair, thinking once again that the hotel room seemed smaller than the tent they'd shared.

Teddy stretched out at Jess's feet. She had pulled out her phone then met his gaze. "I think it's safe enough to have Doug meet us here, don't you agree?"

"Of course. I trust your family. But make sure he doesn't drive one of the SUVs that has your ranch logo on the side."

"Good point." She shook her head as she entered the number. After a moment, she said, "Hey, Doug. How was Hawaii?" There was a pause as he answered. Then her voice rose in surprise. "You're ten minutes from Cody? How did you get here so fast?" Another pause. "Yes, we're at the Lumberjack Inn. See you soon." She lowered the phone. "Doug will be here in a few minutes."

"I heard." Logan wondered if Doug had even unpacked his suitcase from his trip. "I hope Maya isn't upset."

"About Doug helping us? Never." Jess shook her head. "She's not like that. Maya would want us to find this gunman ASAP."

He'd almost forgotten that Maya Sullivan now Bridges had worked as a cop in Cheyenne. No wonder the Sullivans took incidents like this in stride. Most women would be panicking at the idea of being targeted by a gunman.

But not Jess. She was cool under pressure.

He turned to rummage through his backpack. If they were heading back up the mountain at some point, he wanted to be sure his gear was ready to go. He pulled several items out, making sure to spread any wet clothing out near the room's heater to dry.

The knock on their door came five minutes later. He shot over to press his eye up to the peephole to verify who was out there, before standing back to open the door.

"Hi, Logan. Jess." Doug Bridges shook his hand. He'd first met Doug back in January when the guy had paid Logan to take evidence to the state crime lab. Doug had hired Maya to help find his kidnapped sister, and they were successful in finding Emily. Logan then worked with him a month later when Chase had needed backup. In both instances, Logan's role had been minor, just flying from point A to point B.

This was the first time he needed Doug's help on a personal level.

"Thanks for coming." Jess gave her brother-in-law a quick hug. Teddy wagged his tail until Doug bent to give the K9 some attention too. "We've managed to get ourselves in a bit of trouble."

"So I heard." Doug's tone was wry. "Care to fill me in?"

Logan decided to take the lead. "It started with me accepting a request to be flown from Cheyenne to the base of Cedar Mountain." He went on to explain about the piece of plane he'd seen and his decision to let Jessica know. "Teddy alerted near the passenger seat of the plane, and that's when I found the glove."

"We believe Craig Benton, Logan's charter client, was transporting drugs. Or components of drugs," she clarified. "Teddy's been trained on all of them."

"I remember." Doug gave an encouraging nod. "Go on."

When he reached the part when shots were fired at them, Doug's expression hardened. "You weren't hit?"

"We're fine," Jess said. "But it was bad when he tried to shoot down our plane. Thankfully, Logan is a highly skilled pilot and managed to land without incident."

He shouldn't have been touched by her praise. Logan quickly finished the story, ending with Ethan Dover's death and their theory of the overdose being set up to look accidental rather than intentional murder.

"A bit of trouble is putting it mildly," Doug

drawled. "You're smack dab in the middle of this mess."

"It wasn't on purpose," Logan protested. "But you're right. The end result is that big red targets are etched on our backs. This Benton guy and his pals seem to think we know more than we do."

"Although, we're learning more by the minute," Jessica added. "Ethan Dover was murdered for a reason. The only thing that makes sense is if he had started to snoop around about Ella's death, which was also supposedly"—she used air quotes around the word *supposedly*—"a drug overdose."

"Why would he bother to do that now after eight years?" Doug looked skeptical. "I would think he'd moved on with his life."

"Not as much as you'd think," Jess said. "He never got married or started a family." She flushed as if realizing the same could be said about her and Logan. He knew his reasons for not dating were tangled up in his feelings for Jess. Her reasons for staying single were murky. She shrugged. "I don't know Ethan that well anymore, but from our brief interactions at the general store, I got the impression he was a bit of a loner."

"Maybe Ethan learned something new recently," Logan said. "We don't know how long Benton and his guys have been hanging out near Cedar Mountain, but I have a feeling it hasn't been that long."

Doug regarded them silently for a moment. Then he let out a sigh. "The best way to figure out what is going on with this guy is to head back up there."

"I agree, and Teddy can help by tracking the scent of drugs and/or gun powder. That should help us zero in on the correct location." Jessica straightened. "How soon can we head out?"

"Hold on, we need other law enforcement officers to come along." He shot Doug an exasperated look. "Come on, you can't imagine the three of us can pull this off. What about the feds? Or DEA agents?"

"I'll get in touch with Griff Flannery from the FBI." Doug pulled out his phone. "I'm the closest thing to a DEA agent in the area. My current role is that of a criminal investigator for the state of Wyoming, but my boss is trying to change that to include a broader jurisdiction. Sounds like he has support from the FBI office."

"Really?" Jess sounded surprised. "What does Maya think about that?"

"She's fine with whatever I'd like to do. Especially since it hasn't happened yet." Doug grinned wryly and tapped a button on his phone. "But if this ends up being the big drug bust that I think it is, that will likely seal the deal. It's not good that highly potent drugs are finding their way into our cites."

Logan dropped down onto the edge of the bed, listening as Doug connected with the FBI office in Cheyenne. He was slightly reassured that others would be going along with them on this trip. Yet it would also take Agent Flannery a while to get there. Even if he chose to come by plane. Which now that Logan thought about it was the better option.

A glance at his watch had him doing the math. The hour was going on three in the afternoon, so the earliest they could get strike out to head back up to the mountain was first thing in the morning.

He could only hope and pray the trip back to the wilderness wouldn't turn out to be their last.

<h1 style="text-align:center">11</h1>

J ess was impressed at how Doug managed to get the FBI agent from Cheyenne along with a game warden and several local police officers from Cody, including Sergeant Wayne Carter, to accompany them to the mountain.

"I'm surprised the local cops will have jurisdiction outside of Cody," she said when Doug had finished with the arrangements.

"They'll be deputized by the FBI as adjunct officers." Doug shrugged. "They do that quite a bit out here. I would rather involve cops I know we can trust than adding the sheriff's deputies I've never met to the list."

Jess knew Doug was still upset at how he'd learned about a dirty cop being involved in his sister's kidnapping back in January. So she didn't blame him for being leery about adding unknown cops to the list. Back then, drugs had been the underlying reason for Emily's kidnapping.

The arrests Doug had made back then may have slowed things down, but it was obvious the drug trade had been rejuvenated by Benton and his pals. And Ethan Dover had paid the price.

She really wished she knew why he was murdered.

"I hope we have enough people," Logan said. When she looked at him in surprise, he scowled. "We don't have any idea how many bad guys are up there."

"Speaking of getting up there, what are your thoughts?" Doug asked. "Flying in might attract attention."

Logan grimaced. "I have a plane we can use, but I agree that would be like announcing our arrival. I think we should drive to the Cabin Creek Campsite and go in by foot from there."

"It will be a long hike," Jess said. "But I agree, that's probably better than flying."

"Okay, then." Doug rose. "Now that we have everything set up to go for early tomorrow morning, I'm heading back to the ranch." He paused, glancing at Jess. "Unless you think I need to stick around here?"

"No need," she hastened to reassure him. "I'm sure we're safe."

Logan frowned but didn't offer an argument.

"You have my number if you need anything." Doug bent to give Teddy a pat. "And the local police will be on high alert too."

She didn't bother pointing out that there would be only two officers on duty overnight. She and Logan had Teddy as an extra layer of protection. "Thanks again, Doug. I will feel better once we get back on that mountain to find this guy."

"I just hope we find him before he finds us," Logan said, following Doug to the door.

"That reminds me, I'll need you to bring a handgun from the ranch for me to use tomorrow." Jess glanced down at Teddy. "Logan is right that we need to be prepared for the worst-case scenario. He has a weapon, but I didn't bring one along."

Doug hesitated. "I assume you know how to use it?"

She arched a brow. "Do you really think Maya and Chase wouldn't make sure we could all hit what we're aiming at?"

"Okay, okay." Doug grinned. "I know Maya is a crack shot and so is Chase. I should have known the rest of you would be well versed in using firearms too."

"Thanks." She sank back down onto the bed as

Doug left and Logan closed the door and shot the deadbolt home.

"I'm not sure this is a good idea," Logan said.

She suppressed a sigh. "We've been over this Logan. Doug has involved several law enforcement agencies as support for the mission. Besides, what's the alternative? This guy will only continue to target us if we don't put an end to this."

"I know." He sighed. "I just wish there was a way to add more safety measures."

That gave her an idea. "You know, Teddy's K9 vest is made of Kevlar. And of course we made sure all the dogs have them. After what happened to Chase in February, we added bullet-resistant vests to our supply of search and rescue gear too." She pulled out her phone to send Doug a text. "I'm sure Doug would bring extras for us."

Logan perked up. "That would make me feel better."

"Great." She glanced around the seemingly minuscule hotel room. After their late lunch, she wasn't hungry for dinner. But she needed to feed Teddy, so she reached for her pack. She filled his collapsible food and water dishes. Teddy sat staring at her as she did so, but he didn't go for the food until she gave him the signal.

"Go ahead, Teddy. Eat." She pointed at the dishes.

Teddy ate with enthusiasm, although he didn't scarf his food as quickly as some of her siblings' K9s did. When he finished eating, he lapped at the water, then went to stand by the door.

"Hold on, I'm going with you." Logan grabbed his coat.

She slipped her jacket on without protest. Was it just earlier that morning that the gunman had fired on them? It seemed like eons ago, rather than hours.

"We'll use that strip of land between the parking lot of the hotel and the drugstore," she said as they headed outside.

"Stick close to me," Logan said.

She nodded as Teddy ran ahead. They kept their K9s on schedule as much as possible just for this reason. Much easier to handle taking their SAR partners out to do their business.

"Get busy, Teddy," she ordered.

The dog didn't need any encouragement. He sniffed around for the perfect spot, then did his thing. She hurried forward to clean up after him. "Good boy, Teddy."

Teddy wagged his tail. Normally, she'd spend some time playing, a.k.a. training, with him, but he'd done enough work for the day.

And they had a long day ahead of them tomorrow.

Logan scanned their surroundings as he waited.

When she and Teddy were ready, they headed inside.

Now what? she thought as Logan once again locked the door behind them. The idea of watching television didn't appeal to her. Yet there wasn't anything else to do, so she reached for the remote.

A wide yawn hit her hard. Logan noticed and nodded.

"I'm exhausted too." He gestured to the bed he was sitting on. "I'm ready to get some sleep. Do you want to use the bathroom first?"

"Yes, thanks. That sounds good to me." She clicked the remote off. Ten minutes later, she was stretched out on the double bed with Teddy lying beside her. She'd decided to sleep in her clothes, just in case they had to leave in a hurry.

Logan did the same.

She didn't expect to fall asleep right away and found herself listening intently to both Teddy's snoring and Logan's deep breathing. The soft mattress and pillow beneath her head should have been enough to help her relax.

They weren't.

She turned from one side to the next, then did her best to still her mind with prayer.

The next thing Jess knew, Teddy was growling. She blinked in the darkness, trying to remember where she was and what had caught her K9's attention. Sometimes the dog let out little yips while sleeping, his little paws moving as he dreamed.

But this was different.

"What's wrong?" Logan asked, his voice groggy with sleep.

"I'm not sure." She swung out of the bed. Teddy's head was up, his ears pricked forward as he seemed focused on the window.

"I'll take a look." Logan stood and kept to the side as he lifted the edge of the curtain just enough to peer out.

She slid her feet into her boots. Teddy jumped off the bed and stood in front of her. "See anything?"

"Nothing alarming." Logan let the edge of the curtain drop. "But let's stay clear of the window for a while."

She moved toward the hotel room door, wondering if something out in the hallway had caught Teddy's attention. A split second later, the window shattered beneath the force of a bullet.

"Jess!" Logan shouted, as she ducked and covered Teddy's body with hers.

"I'm fine." Her voice was hoarse as she reached for her phone, intending to call 911. But another gunshot followed the first, negating that idea. The window was already broken, but she heard the thud of the bullet hitting the drywall on the other side of the room. "We need to get out of here."

"I know." Logan lunged across the bed, grabbed his gun, then rolled off to the other side. He shoved his feet into his shoes and joined her at the door. "Stay back in case someone is out there."

That possibility hadn't occurred to her. "Heel, Teddy." The dog obediently hovered near her side.

Logan looked out the peephole, then yanked the door open. Seconds later, they were heading down the hall toward the lobby.

The clerk looked up, earbuds in her ears. She quickly removed them, and asked, "Is something wrong?"

"Call 911 and report shots fired. Hurry!" Logan snapped when the clerk simply gaped at them.

When she didn't move fast enough, he leaned over the desk, snagged the phone receiver, and made the call himself. Jess hovered beside him, with Teddy between them, warily eyeing the front door for a sign of the shooter's accomplice.

"Get behind the desk," Logan said when he'd finished making the call.

"Oh, but . . ." The clerk started to protest, but Logan ignored her.

Jess moved to edge around the main desk. Teddy followed, and Logan came last. The clerk must have realized it was useless to argue, as she cowered in the corner.

A dark figure approached the front door. Jessica's breath froze in her chest as Logan held his weapon in a two-handed grip, aiming at the front door.

Then the sound of police sirens cut through the air. Instantly, the figure in black whirled and took off.

Jess sagged against the desk, her knees weak. Logan shot her a grim glance. She nodded in understanding.

That was too close. And worse, they had no idea how the gunman had found them at the Lumberjack Inn.

She peered at her watch. It was barely four o'clock in the morning. Three hours until they were meeting to head up the mountain.

Clearly, finding and arresting Benton was the only way to end this nightmare once and for all.

Logan hated knowing how close they'd come to being killed in their beds. If not for Teddy's growling, they wouldn't be standing there, waiting for the police to arrive.

And how the dog had known about the gunman was a mystery. Could the dog smell through walls? Or had he heard something? Dogs could hear high-pitched sounds that people couldn't. Too bad Teddy couldn't talk to clue them in.

For now, he was grateful for the K9's keen senses.

A Cody police officer wrenched the lobby door open. "Police!"

Logan quickly lowered his weapon. "Thanks for coming so quickly."

"I'm Jessica Sullivan, and this is Logan Fletcher," Jess said. "I'm not sure if Sergeant Wayne Carter let you know we might be in danger."

"He did." The cop's last name was Norman. "What happened?"

Logan glanced toward the hallway that led to their room. "At least two bullets penetrated the window of our room. We managed to escape long enough to call you. A man dressed in black approached the front door of the lobby but then took off when he heard the sirens."

"Stay back, I'll check it out." Officer Norman looked wary as he edged down the hallway, holding his weapon ready. Logan had a new appreciation for these officers who faced danger with little to no backup.

After the cop disappeared from view, he turned toward Jess. "You'd better call Doug."

She reached for the desk phone with trembling fingers. Teddy stayed close to her side.

The scared-out-of-her-mind clerk had straightened now and looked as if she might argue. Logan shot her a withering look. "Those earbuds prevented you from hearing the gunfire. What if that guy had come in through the front door, huh? You'd be dead."

The blood drained from her face. "I—I didn't know!"

He barely refrained from rolling his eyes. "Of course, you didn't know. If I had known a gunman would show up, I would have called the cops earlier. My point is you made yourself a vulnerable target. Next time, read a book without music."

The clerk covered her face with her hands, making him feel bad for being so blunt. It wasn't right to take his anger and frustration out on her. Then she abruptly glared at him accusingly. "You used different names."

"Yeah. And now you know why." Logan wasn't about to apologize.

Officer Norman returned a few minutes later, his expression grim. "I'm glad you were able to get out without being hurt. There's no sign of the gunman now. My partner, Heath Anderson, is outside checking the area. I also notified Sergeant Carter. He wanted me to tell you he's on his way."

"Thanks." Logan felt better at hearing there was no sign of the gunman. Yet he wished he could have gotten a better look at the guy. He turned to the desk clerk. "Do you have a camera outside? One pointing at the front door?"

"Yes." She sniffed and wiped away her tears. Clearly still badly shaken, she stepped up and logged into the computer. A moment later, she pulled up the camera screen. "Just the one. The owner had it put in a few months ago."

"Probably after Doug and Maya had been targeted by gunfire outside," Jess murmured. "Although the owner could have sprung for more than one."

Logan privately agreed. He watched the screen as the clerk backed up the video. She cued it up, then stepped back to give him room. "Just press the play button."

"Thanks." He was about to use the mouse to click the screen, then glanced at her expectantly. "Sorry, I didn't catch your name."

"Debra. Debra Walworth."

"Thanks, Debra." He slowed the speed of the video so that he wouldn't miss anything. There was no movement outside the door for several long minutes, then he saw the figure in black step from the shadows. Narrowing his gaze, he watched as the guy dressed in black, complete with a black face mask, reach forward as if to open the door, then abruptly stop. There was no sound to accompany the video, but Logan assumed that was when the gunman heard the police sirens.

Two seconds later, the guy was gone. Logan backed it up and played the video again. Other than a pair of dark eyes and pale skin around the face mask, the gunman didn't have any identifying features. He watched the video two more times, it was barely six seconds total, then stopped.

He'd hoped to recognize something about him. But that proved impossible. The mask covered his face to the point it could have been anyone standing out there.

"Do you see anyone else nearby?" Jess peered at the screen over his shoulder. "Could this be the same guy who fired at us?"

"He appears to be alone." He had to admit that was strange. If there was a large drug operation going on, then why not send several bad guys after them? He turned his head, keenly aware that she was close enough to kiss. *An inappropriate thought at an equally inappropriate time*, he silently chided. He needed to stay focused. "Based on the time frame between the gunfire and his showing up at the front door, I believe he was working alone. If there had been two of them, they'd have approached from both sides at the same time. The window and the main doorway." The idea was chilling. They would have been sitting ducks in that hotel room.

"I guess that was good for us, huh?" She briefly rested her forehead on his shoulder, then straightened. "Teddy must have heard something. He woke me from a sound sleep."

"Me too. That dog of yours is the hero of the day." Logan stepped back as Wayne Carter arrived. The sergeant wasn't in uniform, his hair sticking out of his head as if the guy had rolled straight from his bed to respond. "Wayne."

"What happened?" Wayne demanded.

Logan briefed him on the shooting. Debra looked upset when he mentioned she was wearing earbuds and hadn't heard anything. Ignoring her, he finished the update. "There's a camera out front, and we've already reviewed the corresponding video. Unfortunately, the guy is dressed in black and wearing a face mask, so it's not very helpful. All I can say for sure is that he's white and appears to be of average height and weight." *Much like Craig Benton*, he silently added.

"Play it again for me." Wayne crowded in behind the counter to see for himself. Logan hit the triangle button to start the video clip. Wayne sighed as he straightened. "You're right. It's about as helpful as an eleventh toe."

That made Logan grin. "You're right about that. However, there are bullets embedded in the drywall of our room. They may provide some information."

"I'll need a copy of this video," Wayne told Debra. "And obviously the room that was targeted by gunfire is off-limits until we've processed it."

"Of course." Debra looked pale. "I should probably call my boss to let him know about this."

"That reminds me," Jess interrupted. "I'll take Teddy outside so we can search for shell casings."

Wayne considered that for a moment, then shook his head. "No need. By the time I arrived, Heath mentioned he'd found a couple of casings in the parking lot out back. This guy isn't smart enough to pick up his brass, so I'm sure the others aren't far."

Logan nodded. "Two casings are about right. I only heard two shots." That, too, struck him as odd. Why not open fire, showering the room with bullets?

Who were these guys anyway?

"Same," Jess said. "Two shots. By God's grace and Teddy's growling, we were warned ahead of time that something was wrong. We were out of our beds, Logan off to the side of the window while I was near the main door. Miraculously, the bullets whizzed right past both of us, striking the opposite wall."

"I was surprised Teddy growled like that. Can that dog smell through walls or what?" Logan asked.

"I'm sure he heard something," Jess mused. "Although it's interesting that he responded to whatever that was with a low growl. He doesn't usually overreact to strange noises."

Logan considered that for a moment. "Maybe the gunman made some sound he recognized."

"Maybe," Jess agreed.

"Okay, you guys stay here. Which room were you in?" Wayne asked. "I need to check out what's left of it."

Logan gave him the number. Wayne nodded and moved out from behind the desk to cross the lobby. When he reached the hallway, he looked both ways before heading in the correct direction.

Logan gestured toward the plush chairs and sofa overlooking the fireplace. "We may as well sit for a while. We won't be using our room from this point forward." As far as he was concerned, he wasn't going to stay in a hotel again for a very long time.

"Sure." She followed him over but then looked down at Teddy. "He probably needs to go out."

"Okay, hang on. We'll take Wayne or Officer Norman with us." Logan strode quickly down the hall toward their room.

Wayne and Officer Norman stood just inside the doorway, surveying the damage. It looked worse with the lights blazing, shards of glass littering the beds where they'd been sleeping. If Teddy hadn't woken them, he had no doubt they'd have been shot and killed.

The dog too.

While he knew it was a crime scene, he had no intention of leaving their backpacks and outer gear behind. For one thing, they would need it for their trek back up the mountain, especially Teddy's K9 vest. Plus, Jess had other supplies in there. She'd want to feed Teddy breakfast before they headed out.

"Jess needs to take Teddy outside, and I'd like a police escort." He reached for their coats and then the backpacks. "The gunman may not have gone far enough for my peace of mind."

"Okay." Wayne frowned but didn't argue when he gathered their personal items together. "Technically, those should stay."

"Not happening." Logan lifted his chin to the small holes in the wall. "Those bullets are the only evidence you'll need." He stared at the broken glass for a minute. It was strange that the gunman had known their exact location. And if so, why had he fired through the window rather than going through the lobby? "There's no reason for us not to have our things."

"I guess you're right. The crime scene techs have been getting enough of a workout over these past few days." Wayne shook his head as he reached for

Jessica's backpack to lighten Logan's load. "Feels like January with Doug Bridges searching for his missing sister all over again."

Logan nodded in understanding. Cody didn't normally have this level of crime. None of the cities in Wyoming did. It was one of the biggest reasons people flocked to the area.

And it was also why these drug dealers had chosen a remote area to produce their illegal trade. If that's what they were up to.

He followed Wayne back to the lobby.

"Thanks." Jess took her pack from Wayne, setting it on the chair. Then she reached for her coat. Teddy stood staring at the front door as if willing it to open. Or maybe willing him and Jess to read his mind about his need to go out. The dog was smart, no doubt about that. Logan drew on his coat.

Wayne led the way, opening the door for Jess and Teddy.

The two police cruisers and an SUV sat outside the front of the hotel. Hopefully, they were enough of a deterrent for the gunman.

"Get busy, Teddy," Jess said. The dog trotted over to lift his leg on the squat bushes lining the front of the property.

"I take it you've called Doug?" Wayne asked.

"I did, yes." Jess watched her dog. "I told him there was no rush, but I suspect he'll show up soon.

At this rate, we should plan on heading out at first light."

"This trip is likely to be full of peril." Wayne's expression was grim. "We'll need to be on full alert."

That's putting it mildly, Logan thought. But he didn't comment. What could he say? There was no getting around the fact that Teddy was their best chance of finding this guy. And there's no way in the world Jess would let the dog go with anyone else.

All he could do was hope and pray that by this time tomorrow the danger would be over for good.

12

Jess settled into the sofa across from the fireplace in the lobby and hugged Teddy close. She knew Wayne was right about the looming danger. Her primary concern was her dog. And Logan.

Logan strode to the front desk. "Debra, any chance we can get some coffee? For the police officers too?"

"Oh, ah, sure." Debra looked flustered. "There's a coffeemaker in the back. I'll brew a pot."

"Thank you. We'd really appreciate it." Logan turned away to join her at the sofa. They both watched the fire for several long moments until he asked, "How long will it take Doug to get here?"

"It's a forty-five-minute drive, and that doesn't take into account the time he'll need to pack our gear, including the bullet-resistant vests I've asked him to bring along." She shrugged and eyed her watch. "It's going on five in the morning now. I'm sure he'll get here as soon as possible."

Logan nodded. "I guess there's no rush. We need to wait for daylight before we head up the mountain anyway."

She glanced outside to the barest hint of dawn creeping over the horizon. Her stomach rumbled with hunger, and she knew she'd have to feed Teddy soon too. She hadn't remembered seeing a room service menu, but the Hitching Post wasn't far. It would be good for all of them to have a big breakfast before hitting the road.

"Here you go." Debra brought them two steaming cups of coffee.

"Thank you." Jess gratefully sipped hers.

The clerk stood awkwardly for a moment. "I hate to ask, but my boss wants to know who will be paying for the room damage." She twisted her hands, avoiding their direct gaze. "The extra cash you gave me won't be enough to cover it. I'm hoping you'll give me more, as I'm in enough trouble already."

"I'll gladly pay for the damage," Jess hastily assured her. She reached over to dig in her pack for her wallet. Finding her credit card, she handed it over. "Here, keep this on file to cover the bill. Make sure your boss knows I will need to match the repair invoices with the charges, so I'll expect to see those receipts."

"Oh, thank you." Debra looked relieved. "I'll let him know. I'm really sorry I didn't hear anything."

Jess glanced at Logan, who was frowning about the cost of the repairs. She put a reassuring hand on his arm. Their family had managed to keep the full extent of their wealth a secret, and that wasn't something she was going to explain to him now. Besides, it's not like the shootout was his fault. She smiled at Debra. "We're fine. As Logan said, avoiding earbuds is a habit that's for your own protection."

"Trust me, I won't do that again." Debra turned and hurried back to her post. It was still too early for the other hotel guests to be up and about, but that would change soon.

"We may need a different place for everyone to gather before heading out." She eyed Logan. "I'm hungry."

"Me too." He nodded to where Wayne was standing a few feet away, talking on his phone. "I figure we wait until Doug gets here to regroup."

"Okay." She took another sip of her coffee, set it aside, and stroked Teddy. The dog was good about stretching out and sleeping when the opportunity presented itself. Considering their plans for the day, he deserved all the rest he could get.

Fifteen minutes later, Wayne strode toward them. He sipped from a cup of coffee provided by Debra. "The crime scene techs have arrived, so they'll take control of the room from Burt. I'll need to head home soon to change. I also connected with Doug; he's about ten minutes out."

"Great." She couldn't suppress the flash of relief in knowing Doug would be there soon. "Go ahead and head home. We'll be fine."

"We're planning to eat at the Post," Logan said. "I'm sure Doug will want breakfast, and you're welcome to join us."

"Sounds good." Wayne drained his cup, then tossed it into the garbage. "See you soon."

As Wayne left, the two crime scene techs entered with a tackle box of gear. Logan stood. "I'll show you the room."

Doug walked into the lobby with her brother Shane a few minutes later. Her brother's K9, Bryce, trotted alongside him. She wasn't surprised her brother had brought his dog. Bryce was a great tracker too. Teddy instantly shot to his feet, excited to see his playmate. The two dogs ran around the lobby as Shane approached, his expression was full of concern. "Hey, Jess. Are you okay?"

"Thanks to Teddy, we're not hurt." She hugged Shane, then Doug. Her brother-in-law had become a key member of their family especially since he'd married Maya. "I'm glad you're here." The dogs' antics made her smile. "And that you brought Bryce along."

"Two noses are better than one," Shane said with a grin.

"We stopped to pick up Shane's SUV." Doug nodded at Logan who'd joined them. "We'll take both SUVs to the campground. Griff Flannery and his colleague Jack Rubio flew in last night." There was a hint of apology in Doug's tone. "He used Allen's Air service."

Allen's Air was run by Big Al Regner. He was based out of Laramie and happened to be Logan's biggest competitor. Logan shrugged, unconcerned. "Can't blame them for using what's available."

She wanted to reassure Logan that his business would recover from this brief interruption, but she couldn't make any promises. God would watch over them, but that didn't mean this trip back to the mountains would be easy. They'd need all His strength and support to get through this.

Yet she also believed their lives would get back to normal once they arrested the gunman and found the drugs he might have hidden nearby.

"Bryce, here." Shane's sharp command broke up the dog's playing. The large German shepherd returned to her brother's side, his tongue lolling to one side of his mouth.

"Teddy, heel." Her K9 obeyed too. It wasn't always easy to get the dogs to stop goofing around, but both of them would need all their strength and stamina to navigate the upcoming search.

"We need breakfast," she told her brother. "Teddy too."

"We told Wayne to meet us at the Hitching Post," Logan added.

"I'm game." Doug glanced at his watch. "I'll see if the feds want to join us."

She reached for her pack, but Shane grabbed it from her fingers. The four of them and the two dogs headed to the Post.

The rest of the law enforcement contingent met up with them within fifteen minutes. They were early enough that they could pull together three tables to accommodate everyone. While they'd waited, she and Shane had fed their respective dogs. And they'd give them a chance to get busy when they were finished eating.

"I'd like to say grace," Doug said, once their meals had been served.

The federal agents and the cops glanced at each other curiously but didn't protest. Jess bowed her head and clasped Logan's hand beneath the table. He gently squeezed it. She was glad Doug had taken the lead on the prayer.

"Dear Lord, we ask You to bless this food. We

also ask for Your strength and guidance as we set out to find and arrest those who would break the law to harm others. Please offer us safe passage on our journey ahead. Amen."

"Amen," she said. Logan and Shane quickly echoed her sentiment. The rest of the officers didn't say the word but nodded solemnly.

"We'll take all the help we can get," Griff said as he reached for the salt and pepper.

"And then some," Wayne added.

As they ate, they discussed strategy. Which basically consisted of breaking into teams to broaden their search. Logan provided detailed coordinates related to where they'd found the plane debris. Two game wardens would be joining their search team as well, meeting up with them at the Cabin Creek Campsite.

"The game wardens, Kevin Tinley and Eddie Marsh, are bringing horses," Doug informed them. "They're going to try to provide an extra layer of coverage for the rest of us who will be on foot."

"We should have brought our horses," Shane muttered.

"I considered it," Doug agreed. "But we're counting on Bryce and Teddy doing the work. It would be harder for us to follow the dogs on horseback."

"I'm fine with hiking." Jess shot Shane an exasperated glance. "We've done this zillions of times before."

"Yeah, yeah." Shane sighed. "I'm game."

It was a full hour later by the time they'd finished eating and were heading up to the campground. She and Logan rode with Doug, who had taken the lead on this endeavor. Shane drove the SUV behind them, with the feds and the others trailing behind.

She glanced at Logan who had insisted on going along with her and Teddy. She had a feeling he planned to stick close to her side.

Two green game warden trucks and a horse trailer were waiting in the parking lot by the time they arrived. Jess let Teddy out of the back of Doug's SUV and instructed him to get busy.

He obliged. She cleaned up his mess, then joined Logan and Doug. Shane was taking care of Bryce too. While they waited, they geared up, strapping on their vests under their jackets. Doug gave her a handgun that he'd gotten from the ranch. She double-checked the weapon and the ammo before putting it in her pocket. Lastly, she added the new earpiece radios that Doug had brought along. She wasn't used to wearing the electronic device but was grateful to have a way to connect with the others if needed.

Doubts crept in as the rest of the law enforcement officers showed up. There were so many of them that she was afraid the bad guys would see them coming from miles away. Even if they split up, they'd be in contact with each other via radio where the sound of their voices could easily be heard.

"I'm not sure about this," she whispered to Logan. "It's going to be impossible to sneak up on these guys."

"Hopefully, they won't know we're coming." Logan glanced at her, then shrugged when she gave him a skeptical look. "Okay, I see your point. The problem is that they're armed and dangerous."

"I know." She sighed. "I just hope this trip isn't in vain."

He nodded in agreement, then they stepped forward to hear Doug's instructions. The two game wardens stood near their horses as Doug spread a topographical map of the area over the hood of his SUV.

"This is our target area." He tapped the coordinates Logan had provided. "But we believe the actual location is a little north and east of here. We'll be in three groups, two with K9s. The game wardens will help cover us from either side."

"I'm going with Logan, Jessica, and Teddy," Doug said. "Griff, I'd like you and Jack Rubio to stick with Shane and Bryce." He turned to the local cops.

"Wayne, you take Burt and Jeff to this area here. Any questions?"

"Nope." Eddie Marsh, the older of the two game wardens, grabbed his horse's reins and vaulted into the saddle. Kevin Tinley mirrored his movements.

Jess looked through her pack, making sure she had water and enough first aid supplies for Teddy if he should need it. Then she was ready go to.

She glanced at Logan before pouring some water into a collapsible dish for Teddy. She offered it to her dog, who lapped the water. Then she knelt beside him. "Are you ready to search? Are you?" She injected enthusiasm in her tone. "Search for peppers. Peppers, Teddy. Search!" She'd considered using the search terms for both gold and peppers but decided to stick with the more important one.

Knowing Teddy, he would not hesitate to let her know if he smelled the gunman or caught a whiff of someone carrying a weapon.

Her K9 lifted his head to the air and sniffed for long minutes. Then he trotted into the woods, darting between several large trees. She hurried to catch up. As she covered the rocky terrain with Teddy, she sent up a quick prayer, tagging on to the one Doug had given prior to breakfast.

Lord Jesus, cover us with Your protection and love!

LOGAN FOLLOWED Jess and Teddy as they moved swiftly through the forest. He shouldn't have been surprised the dog seemed to be taking them up along the same path they'd used yesterday. Maybe it was the fact that they'd left some of their scent behind. Their footprints could be easily seen in the areas that were still covered in snow, but other areas of the forest floor held only rocks and twigs.

It made him wonder if the gunman had used the same path. Although if that was the case, he wasn't sure why the guy hadn't just taken them out of the picture while they were still in the woods.

Behind him, Doug was advising the group to stay radio silent unless there was something to report. Instantly, the radio chatter in his earpiece went quiet. He was glad Doug had issued the order, as he'd found the chatter distracting.

Jess, on the other hand, appeared single-minded in working with Teddy. He didn't like the idea of her taking the lead, but he understood the dog was their most important asset.

He had faith in Shane's Bryce too. He'd found it interesting that the Sullivan family used the same search terms for their K9s. Must be part of the cross-training Jess had mentioned. As Jess had gotten Teddy revved up to search, Shane had done the same with Bryce.

Having two highly trained search dogs was a

recipe for success. So why couldn't he shake the feeling of impending doom hanging over him?

Lack of sleep may be a contributing factor. While he'd appreciated Doug's prayer, he didn't have a lot of practice in reaching out to their heavenly Father for support and guidance. And really, why would God listen to him?

When, not if, they survived this, he would ask Jessica about which church she and her family attended. The way they leaned on their faith to get through times of trouble was humbling. And it made him realize he had a lot to learn.

As he pressed himself to keep up with Jess and Teddy, he swept his gaze over their surroundings. They weren't deep enough into the woods to be anywhere close to the area where they'd found the plane debris, but he wasn't taking any chances.

Glancing behind him, he was reassured that Doug appeared to be on high alert too.

After forty minutes, Jess stopped to give Teddy a rest. He and Doug flanked her on each side as she sat on a log and encouraged Teddy to stretch out beside her.

"Good boy," she murmured, stroking his black fur. The dog didn't appear as short of breath as she was, Logan thought, but he didn't mention it.

"He seems to be on a mission," Doug said.

"He has been going faster than I anticipated."

She smiled weakly. "I suspect that's because he loves the search game and is anxious to find peppers."

"Giving Bryce a break," Shane said in Logan's ear.

"Same with Teddy," he responded.

Jess glanced up at him. "I figured we were still on radio silence."

"It's fine," Doug waved a hand. "I don't mind occasional updates, but in the beginning, these guys were chattering worse than a group of high schoolers."

Logan nodded. "I thought so too." He consulted his compass. "We're on the right track, but we still have a few miles to go."

"We'll get there." Doug grinned. "I'm just glad it's not snowing."

Logan had heard about the blizzard rescue Doug and Maya had pushed through when they'd tracked his missing sister to an isolated cabin in the woods. He had to admit that while this mission they'd embarked on was dangerous, the weather conditions were better.

After ten minutes, Jess stood and began going through the now familiar routine. In his ear, he heard Doug give a brief update. "Rest time over."

"Roger that," Shane replied.

After providing Teddy with some water, Jess got

him excited about the search. "Are you ready? Search for peppers!"

Teddy eagerly attacked the trail, sniffing intently as he continued heading toward the coordinates he'd given Doug. They were fifteen minutes into the walk when Teddy abruptly veered toward the left.

Jess quickly followed her dog. Logan and Doug scrambled to keep up. He wasn't sure what had captured the dog's attention, but it occurred to him that Teddy may be taking them on a more direct route.

Yesterday, they'd taken an alternate path once they'd spotted the hunting shanty, crossing the creek and heading more south than east.

He turned and glanced at Doug who nodded encouragingly. Logan understood he trusted the Sullivan K9s implicitly.

Teddy had saved their lives more than once, so Logan strove to shake off the nagging concern. They could do this.

The gunman was no match for the numerous law enforcement officers who were spread out along the mountainside. As he searched the area, he found it a bit unnerving that he didn't see anyone nearby.

That was the point, he reminded himself. Doug had purposefully spread them out to cover more ground. Far enough so they wouldn't overlap their efforts.

And Doug had arranged for Shane and Bryce to approach the coordinates from the opposite direction with hopes of pinching Benton and his cohorts in crime somewhere in the middle.

A good plan that he hoped would work.

Teddy pushed through the brush. Jess was doing an admirable job in keeping pace with her energetic K9. Logan kept some distance between them in case something caused them to abruptly turn to head back down.

He scanned the wilderness again. This was about the time bears began to emerge from their months' long hibernation. They didn't need that on top of what they already faced.

The game wardens hadn't issued any bear or other wildlife warnings, so he told himself to relax. Yet he had to admit, hiking in silence, even while trying to be on alert for danger, was wreaking havoc with his imagination.

The morning dragged on. Jess took breaks every forty minutes, and after the third break, he could tell Teddy was getting tired. "Maybe we should take a longer break," he suggested. "I don't want Teddy to get hurt."

Doug shrugged. "I'll do whatever Jess thinks is best for her dog."

"How close are we to the target location?" Jess asked.

He sat beside her and double-checked their co-ordinates. "We're making really good time. I esti-mate we're only thirty minutes away. Maybe less."

"Then let's keep going." Jess stroked Teddy's fur. He rested his head between his paws and closed his eyes. "After I give him a little extra downtime. He seems intent on breaking speed records to reach whatever scent has caught his attention."

"I noticed." Logan smiled at the dog. "A longer break would be good. He deserves it."

"I have protein bars." Doug offered them each one, biting into his. "Water too. We're burning a lot of calories."

"I know. I should have hiked like this in high school," Jess joked as she bit into her bar.

Logan wanted to tell her she was beautiful in high school but held his tongue. His reasons for dating Ella had been shallow, something he'd for-ever regret. But he couldn't change the past.

"Okay, let's do this." Jess rose, stretched, then poured some of her water into Teddy's collapsible bowl. The dog didn't hesitate to jump to his feet. He lapped the offered water, then held Jess's gaze as she instructed him to search.

Teddy once again set out at a brisk pace. Logan heard Jessica's low groan as she pushed herself to follow. He and Doug continued trailing behind them.

After about fifteen minutes, he momentarily lost sight of Jess behind a trio of evergreen trees. With a frown, he quickened his pace, glancing back to make sure Doug had noticed.

He was tempted to call out to her, but they were close enough to the coordinates that he didn't want to draw unwanted attention. He listened intently but didn't hear Teddy bark in an alert.

Pushing himself, he broke into a jog to reach the evergreens. As he rounded them, he spotted Jessica and Teddy about fifty yards ahead.

Teddy was moving fast again, his nose sweeping the ground. Logan's pulse kicked up as he realized they were likely close to Benton's hiding place. Yet he still didn't see any buildings, not even a dilapidated hunting shanty.

One minute Jess was walking beside Teddy, the next she vanished. The dog, too, seemed to slip out of sight.

What in the world?

"Jess!" Her name came out in a choked cry.

"What?" Doug asked from behind him.

Logan didn't answer as he ran forward to cover the distance between them. Then he was forced to an abrupt stop when he realized he was on top of a ridge.

Heart thundering in his chest, he stared down at the crevasse below. It wasn't as far down as he'd initially thought, maybe ten feet. Enough to cause broken bones, or worse, but as he stood there, he wasn't sure whether to be relieved or horrified that he didn't see any sign of Jess or Teddy.

Doug scrambled up beside him. "Where is she?" he asked.

Logan shook his head, then dropped to his knees and pointed to a smooth path in the snow that may have been made by Jessica's butt as she slid down the side. "This looks recent to me."

"Yes." Doug knelt beside him, and together they scanned the area below. He imagined Jessica's dark blue coat and her hat and Teddy's fluorescent vest. The smooth path ended at the bottom of the ridge near a tall tree, and he thought he saw footprints leading away from the area. He wasn't reassured.

"We have to get down there," he said in a low voice to Doug.

"Okay." Doug quickly put the rest of the team on alert. "Let's go."

Logan sat on the edge of the ridge and slid down the side on his butt, the same way Jessica had done. He had to believe she'd somehow snagged Teddy to take him down with her, knowing her, likely shielding the dog with her body.

But as he hit the bottom with a jarring thud, he didn't see any sign of them.

Where had they gone?

He pushed himself upright and started forward. Then he stopped as the tiny hairs rose on the back of his neck. There were more than just one set of footprints in the snow. Jess and Teddy weren't alone.

He felt sick at the realization that Jessica and Teddy may have literally fallen right into Benton's lap.

13

The minute Jess had crested the hill, she realized her mistake. Teddy had stopped for a reason. They were atop a bluff. Her foot slipped, and she went down hard on her butt. She grabbed Teddy at the last minute, hauling him onto her lap as she slid down the embankment. Sliding was better than falling, the way her youngest sister, Kendra, had nearly six months ago. Kendra had broken several bones as a result.

Hitting the bottom, she'd quickly released Teddy to scramble to her feet. She tested her arms and legs, realizing with relief that God had been watching over. She wasn't hurt.

Teddy began to growl just as a masked man stepped out from behind a tree. He was several yards away, but there was no mistaking the gun he held in his hand.

"Get up." His voice was low and harsh. "Now. Or I'll shoot you and the dog where you're standing."

She didn't doubt this man had lethal intent. She couldn't see his facial features beyond the black face mask he wore, but she figured he must be Craig Benton. She gave Teddy the hand signal to heel, fearing if the dog alerted, the masked man might shoot.

Keeping Teddy close was somewhat selfish on her part. Yet she didn't see much of an alternative.

At least, not yet.

She obeyed his command, closing the distance between them while debating her options. If she tried to make a run for it, he was close enough to shoot without missing. And she couldn't easily protect Teddy while running. Their vests offered some reinforcement, but she'd heard from Maya that being struck by a bullet at close range while wearing a vest hurt like crazy.

And the impact could cause internal bleeding. Especially for a dog.

"Hurry," the masked man said curtly. Using the tip of his gun, he gestured to a crevasse in the side of the mountain.

A chill snaked down her spine. If she wasn't staring at the opening mostly hidden behind the trees, she'd never have noticed it. Was that where Benton had been hiding all this time? With a sense of dread—she didn't love tight spaces—Jess moved through the opening. There was just enough room for Teddy to squeeze in beside her.

"Keep that dog quiet, and if he makes the slightest move toward me, I'll kill him." The masked man's hard, flat tone convinced her he wasn't joking.

"He's not a trained attack dog," she lied. Teddy would absolutely attack if she gave the command, but she didn't want to risk this guy hurting her K9. "He's trained to track scents, that's all."

"I know. I've watched you." When she slowed and turned to stare at him, he lifted the gun. "Keep moving."

Swallowing hard, she did. The interior of the cave was large enough that they could walk upright, but it was also narrow. So much so that it felt as if the walls were closing in on her. Not good. She couldn't afford to suffer a bad case of claustrophobia. Determined to stay in control, she did her best to take slow, deep breaths to calm her racing heart.

Yet the deeper they went into the cave, the more she worried that Logan and Doug wouldn't be able to find her. Would they notice that crevasse in the wall behind the trees and guess that's where she and Teddy had gone?

Would they realize she'd been taken against her will?

She reached a part of the tunnel that was so narrow she had to let Teddy go through first. Her K9 must have sensed her fear because he stayed close while remaining quiet.

Ironic that their early morning search had in fact led them to their quarry. But not in the way she'd hoped.

They'd depended too much on Teddy's tracking ability, which had been hindered in part due to the gunman standing down in the ravine. She had no doubt Teddy would have found the cave.

Too bad the masked gunman had found them first. Maybe he'd even come out of the cave in time to hear her sliding on her fanny down the side of the ravine.

She mentally kicked herself for not paying closer attention to the reason Teddy had stopped like that, but there was no time for regrets. Her new goal was to stay alive long enough for Logan and Doug to find her.

While doing her best to avoid getting shot.

They seemed to walk through the cave forever, until finally the corridor widened into a room. There were boxes stacked along the wall, and from the way Teddy sniffed the base of them, then sat to look at her without barking, made her realize they held drugs. Or more likely, the components used to make synthetic drugs.

Again, she gave Teddy the hand signal to heel. The dog quickly returned to her side. She eyed the masked man warily. "I assume you're Craig Benton?"

"I knew that pilot had come back to find me for a reason." Disgust laced his tone. "He should have just minded his own business."

"Logan didn't come back to this area because of you." Jess frowned, hoping to buy time by keeping him talking. "He saw a piece of a tail fin that may have been from my parents' plane wreck from a crash that happened five years ago. We returned to find it, to take it back with us, not to search for you." She gestured to the cave and the subsequent boxes stacked along the far side. "If you'd have just left us alone, we wouldn't be standing here right now. None of this would have happened."

He said nothing for a moment, then shrugged. "Maybe not. But now that you're here, I have little choice but to remove you as a threat." He lowered the barrel of his gun toward Teddy. "And him too."

"Listen, I don't care about your drug business." Another lie, but she didn't think God would mind. "There's no reason to kill us."

"It's too late; you shouldn't have come back here." His tone hardened. "And how did you know what was in those boxes?"

She inwardly winced at her second mistake in a matter of minutes. She really needed to stay focused! Striving for a casual tone, she shrugged. "I don't know what's in them, but it must be something illegal, or you wouldn't be standing there holding a gun on me."

"It's that dog of yours, isn't it?" He glared at Teddy.

"No, Teddy didn't alert on anything. He would have barked if he'd caught the scent of drugs." Another lie, and there were so many now that she was losing count. She tried to think of a way to defuse the situation but was coming up empty.

How long would it take for Logan and Doug to find her?

Too long, based on the way the masked man was glaring at her.

When he lifted his wrist to look at his watch, she realized why they were standing there. He was waiting for someone.

She cast a quick glance around the cave, desperate for a way out. If others were on the way, she couldn't wait for Logan or Doug.

There was a shadow behind the stack of boxes that could be another tunnel. Would it lead deeper into the mountainside?

Should she make a run for it?

Without giving herself time to think it through,

she gave Teddy the hand signal for go as she darted toward the shadow. Her movement must have caught her captor off guard because the guy didn't shoot at them as she and Teddy disappeared down the tunnel.

It was dark, so she had to keep one hand on the wall as she ran.

Within seconds, she was proven wrong. A crack of gunfire echoed from behind her. She'd expected it, so she did her best to ignore the sound while continuing to move farther into the cavern. The darkness would hide Teddy more than her, and that was okay.

When her head smacked into something hard, she realized the tunnel was narrowing. Not good. What if she ended up in some dead-end tunnel with nowhere to hide?

Forcing herself to go slower, she felt along the way for an offshoot of what seemed to be the main tunnel. This had to be an old gold or silver mine of some sort. Something they should have considered when they hadn't seen any above ground structures.

For all they knew, they had a full drug operation going on down here.

"You can't escape," the gunman called. His low, raspy voice bounced off the walls in an eerie echo.

She bit back the urge to respond. Maybe all she

was doing was buying more time, but it was better than nothing.

Then she suddenly realized she could see the tunnel up ahead. The darkness wasn't as complete as it had been, which meant the masked man behind her had a flashlight.

Jess pressed forward, hugging the wall, feeling the reassuring presence of Teddy beside her while praying he was wrong. That they would be able to find a way to escape. That this wasn't a dead end.

That she and Teddy wouldn't die down there.

She and her siblings believed in God and everlasting life with Jesus, so she wasn't necessarily afraid to die. But she had regrets. So many regrets.

Primarily not telling Logan how much she cared about him. That she never really blamed him for Ella's overdose. That she was as much at fault as anyone.

Because she'd been jealous of Ella and Logan's relationship.

Yet this wasn't the time to think about that now. She had to keep moving! The tunnel turned to the right, so she slipped around the corner and quickened her pace. After another few feet, the tunnel turned again to the left. She continued following it, praying this would lead to the outside at some point.

Instead, she noticed the faint glow of light emanating from up ahead.

Her heart lodged in her throat. Someone was likely in the next tunnel. Maybe more than one person.

She glanced back over her shoulder. The bouncing light from the flashlight was slowly and surely closing the gap. She reached down, her fingers tangling in Teddy's fur.

They were trapped!

"I DON'T UNDERSTAND where she and Teddy could have gone." The impending sense of doom that had dogged Logan's steps on their way up the mountain had returned in full force as the minutes ticked by without any sign of Jess or Teddy. It was as if they'd disappeared into some sort of time warp.

Something was wrong.

"It could be that Teddy is hot on the scent," Doug said. "Although I can't figure out which direction they went."

"Let's split up and look for her footprints along with Teddy's." The melting snow made tracking difficult. At the bottom of the ravine, they'd found the two sets of footprints, left by Jessica and some unknown person. But since then, they'd found nothing to help them identify where they'd gone.

Logan knew the footprints could have been left the previous day, but he didn't think so. Yet if Jess had crossed paths with the gunman or some other stranger, wouldn't Teddy have let them know?

Not if Jessica had told him to stay quiet. Teddy was well trained and obeyed every one of Jess's commands.

He and Doug split up, moving forward in a V pattern from the bottom of the ravine. He walked slowly, scanning the ground.

But found nothing.

It didn't make any sense. After several long minutes of searching, he turned to retrace his steps back to the bottom of the ravine. This was the last known place where he knew Jess and Teddy had been. Their tracks were obvious.

Then they disappeared as if the pair had been picked up by a helicopter and taken away.

Doug joined him a minute later, his expression equally grim. Then he put his hand up to his radio to put the rest of the team on notice. "Jess and Teddy have vanished, possibly being detained by our gunman. Please stay alert."

"Where are you?" Shane's voice was terse. "I'll bring Bryce your way."

Doug hesitated, then gave the coordinates.

"That's fine if you head over. We'll keep looking and let you know if we find anything. But please be careful, Shane. We don't know how many gunmen are out there."

Hearing Doug's dire statement via his earpiece made Logan feel sick. He'd never felt so helpless in his entire life. Not even after learning of Ella's overdose.

He should have followed Jess more closely. Stayed right on her heels rather than giving her and Teddy room to work.

Even better, he should have insisted on taking the lead rather than leaving it to her and Teddy . . .

"Don't," Doug said quietly. "I know you're wrestling with regrets, but that's no help. Rehashing what you could have done differently is useless. Right now, we need to focus our efforts on finding her."

He was right. Regrets wouldn't change the past. He'd learned that the hard way after Ella's overdose the night after their breakup. Pushing the past aside, Logan took a deep breath and scanned their surroundings for what seemed like the millionth time. Where could she and Teddy have gone? A woman and a dog didn't just disappear into thin air. "I wish Teddy would make some noise so we'd know where to look."

Doug nodded and turned to look at the woods

ahead of them. "I know what you mean. Some of the Sullivan K9s are surprisingly nonvocal. Teddy is one of them. The opposite of Chase's Rocky."

Logan tried to remain calm. Shane and Bryce would be there soon, and he was hopeful that Shane's German shepherd would be able to track Jessica's and Teddy's scent. Without finding additional footprints, he was at a loss as to where to look next.

The sound of a gunshot had him reaching for his gun. Doug did, too, and they instinctively turned so that their backs were together, facing any potential oncoming threat.

"Where did it come from?" Logan asked after a long second.

"I'm not sure." Like him, Doug was sweeping his gaze over the area. "It sounded muffled, like from a silencer."

"Maybe up on the other side of the ridge?" Even as he offered the suggestion, Logan realized that was impossible. They'd have noticed Jess and Teddy scrambling up the side of the mountain.

He stared at the mountainside, noticing for the first time what seemed to be a crack in the rock that was mostly hidden behind the trees. He quickly moved forward, holding his weapon, ready to examine the area.

Up close, he was shocked to realize the crack

was much wider at the base of the mountain. It was more than a crack.

It was a cave!

"Doug!" He used his arm to push the tree branches out of his way to get closer. He swept his gaze over the ground. The opening was too close for snow to have gathered there, exposing potential footprints. Yet, there was no doubt in his mind that Jess and Teddy could have easily gone inside.

Not voluntarily, considering the gunfire. No, he was convinced the gunman must have hidden them away at gunpoint.

"Is that a cave?" Doug sounded surprised as he crossed over to join him.

Logan nodded, putting a finger to his lips. If the bad guys were using it as a hideout, he didn't want to alert them of their presence. "What do you think?" he whispered.

Doug leaned in, listening intently. Logan did the same. He couldn't hear voices, but this had to be where the sound of the gunshot had originated. The walls of the cave, the mountain, and the trees surrounding the opening would have muffled the sound.

"We need to go inside," Logan whispered.

Doug's brow furrowed as he considered the possibilities. He kept his voice low too. "Okay, but someone needs to wait here for Shane and Bryce."

"You should stay and wait for the others." Logan was the least qualified person to go inside, but he refused to stay back. The woman he loved was inside with her K9.

He had to go in.

Logan hovered inside the cave opening, keeping his head down while straining to listen. How far back did this cave go anyway? He felt certain it must have been an abandoned gold or silver mine.

Yet how the gunman and his cohorts had found it was a mystery.

Although it did explain why he hadn't seen a hunting cabin in the vicinity of the area where he'd landed the plane to let Craig Benton out. A big red flag that he would make sure he never ignored again.

Now he realized it had been a makeshift airstrip that had likely been used by several other small charter plane companies. The thought made him wince. How many pilots had been duped by Benton?

And how many were willing participants, satisfied to take the cash while turning a blind eye to the cargo they were carrying?

Once they made it out of this alive, he'd make sure Doug and the others investigated them all. Every single one.

Logan stepped into the cave. Doug snagged his arm. "Wait. You're not a cop," Doug whispered.

Logan shot him a narrow glance and shook free. "Doesn't matter. You provide backup as soon as the others get here. Maybe have them spread out to search for another way inside. This can't be the only opening." He held Doug's gaze for a long moment. "Trust me, we'll be counting on you to bring the cavalry as soon as possible."

Doug clearly wasn't happy but must have understood there was no changing Logan's mind because he sighed and reluctantly nodded. "Okay, fine. But be careful. We'll be right behind you."

"Thanks." He stepped farther into the cave, keeping his hand on the wall for guidance. It was dark, which made him wonder how the gunman was navigating through the cavern. Did he have a flashlight? Or had he simply memorized the layout of the tunnels?

Logan walked as silently and quickly as possible, holding the gun in his right hand down at his side. He tried not to imagine the worst-case scenario. That he wouldn't stumble over Jessica's dead body after the next turn.

He didn't want to believe she was dead.

They were wearing vests, so maybe she'd just been injured. Or had somehow avoided being hit at all.

Teddy? He winced, not even wanting to consider the possibility the gunman had shot the dog. Jess would be inconsolable if that happened.

And she would have taken the bullet herself rather than risk Teddy.

Enough. He pushed the negativity away and focused on the positive. Jess was smart and so was her dog. They'd find a way to survive until help could arrive.

Up ahead, he caught a flash of light that gave him pause. The gunman and Jess? If so, why couldn't he hear anything?

Logan quickened his pace, ducking when he hit a low section of the tunnel. Within a few feet, he was able to stand upright again. The light brightened as he drew closer.

Then he stepped into what looked to be a storage room. He frowned, taking note of the stacked boxes along the far wall. Edging closer, he wasn't surprised to realize they weren't marked in any way with labels.

But the size and shape were very similar to the box Craig Benton had stored behind his seat on the plane. Had the rest of the alleged camping gear contained the same items? Eyeing them now, he realized they must have been stored in the camping equipment because it was clear these boxes hadn't been processed through the post office or any other official transportation service.

He'd done this. Granted, without his knowledge, but still. He felt like an idiot for not realizing his plane was being used to transport drugs. If that was what was contained in the box. Which the more he thought about Teddy's alert in his plane, the more he leaned toward believing that's exactly what was going on here.

But uncovering the exact items stored inside the boxes was a problem for later. Right now, he would continue to follow the light.

Accepting the very real possibility that doing so would take him straight toward the gunman.

He hadn't attended church since he was a child, and he'd known even then that his mother had taken them primarily to get a free meal. He hadn't minded. The pastor's message had gone over his head, but he vaguely remembered a few lines from the Lord's Prayer. Not the whole thing, but the beginning.

He silently recited the words now. *Our Father, whom art in heaven, hallowed by thy name. Thy kingdom come, thy will be done, on earth as it is in heaven.*

That was all he knew, but repeating the opening of the prayer over and over in the back of his mind helped calm his ragged nerves. He wasn't entirely sure what the prayer meant, but he knew that with God's strength he'd get through this.

And so would Jess.

After going another fifty feet, he caught sight of a shadow.

Not a shadow. Teddy! The dog's eyes gleamed in the darkness as the dog bounded toward him. The animal's paws were surprisingly quiet against the tunnel floor.

Dropping to one knee, Logan wrapped his arm around the dog's torso. "Good boy," he whispered near the K9's ear. He didn't dare speak any louder. "Good boy," he repeated, imagining the dog's fur carried the scent of Jess's shampoo.

He took a minute to pocket his weapon. Then he spent another few minutes to double-check that the animal wasn't injured. Beneath his fingers, Teddy's vest felt intact, and he didn't find anything alarming as he ran his fingers up and down the dog's limbs.

Relieved, he hugged the dog again. Then he stood and pulled his gun from his pocket.

There was no sign of Jess, which was concerning. It wasn't normal for Teddy and Jess to be separated. He stared down the tunnel, his mind wrestling with possibilities.

Had the dog sneaked past the gunman?

Or had the guy simply let Teddy go because he'd already silenced Jessica? It made sense to a point.

The dog wasn't a threat. It wasn't as if Teddy could tell the police or other law enforcement officials what had transpired.

Logan stayed where he was, debating his next move. There was still nothing but silence from up ahead. And nothing to indicate Doug or Shane or anyone else had come into the cave to back them up.

Glancing down at Teddy, he realized the dog had turned so that his nose was facing the faint light at the end of the tunnel. Teddy moved forward, then turned to look back at Logan as if to ask *Aren't you coming?*

The dog's pleading gaze was enough to cement his decision. Logan stepped forward too. He would follow Teddy back to where Jess was being held.

He wasn't leaving this cave without her.

14

———

J ess stumbled forward when the masked man pressed the muzzle of his gun into her back. A second man had come from the opposite direction, leaving her nowhere to run or hide. The newcomer, who was shorter than the man behind her, was also armed and wore a black ski mask. The first gunman had tied her wrists together with rope, but he hadn't searched her pockets for a weapon.

She was ashamed to admit she'd forgotten about the gun Doug had provided. Stupid move on her part. Now that she was dealing with two gunmen, she thought it was best to wait until she had a better opportunity to use it.

The one bright spot in this mess was that she'd given Teddy the command to get help. Her K9 had managed to slip away, his black coat hiding him in the darkness.

"You better hope that dog of yours doesn't come back," the guy behind her said in a harsh voice. "Because next time, I won't hesitate to shoot him."

She didn't answer. As much as she hoped Teddy had found Logan or Doug or someone else from the law enforcement team, she knew without a doubt Teddy would return. Hopefully with enough help that her beautiful and smart K9 wouldn't be hurt.

"We need to get out of here," the newcomer said. His voice was low and nasal. "The others won't be far behind."

"We'll need to get rid of them, one by one," the guy behind her said. "Moving is out of the question. We have too much product here to leave behind."

"The product can be replaced," the nasal guy said. "The best approach is to kill her, leave her behind, and bug out."

A strange calmness washed over Jess. If these were her last minutes on earth, then she may as well make the most of them.

By taking these guys down with her. At the very least, she could prevent more drugs from being made and sold to innocent people out on the street.

"Do you have any idea how long it will take to replace that product?" the guy behind her demanded. "We're already behind thanks to these idiots."

On the word *idiot*, the guy behind her jabbed his gun into her back.

"I told you; we didn't return because we were suspicious of you. We only came back to get a piece of the plane." She shot the guy a frustrated glance over her shoulder. "You're the idiot for thinking it was more than that."

Another sharp jab to her back made her stumble. Somehow, she managed to stay upright.

She understood their arguing worked in her favor. They were moving deeper into the cave, though. And she didn't much like how the walls were closing in. The air seemed stale, and she could feel her chest tighten with fear.

When they rounded the next corner, though, she saw brighter lights illuminating from a room up ahead. Her heart sank. More bad guys?

How many could she take down before she died?

She strained to listen but couldn't hear anything helpful. She instinctively slowed her steps, which was a mistake. The guy behind her jabbed her with his weapon again.

"Move," he barked.

She straightened her shoulders, twisting her wrists in hopes of loosening the bindings. Reaching her weapon in her right-hand jacket pocket wouldn't be easy considering the guy she believed to be Craig Benton had tied her hands together at her back.

Yet the bulky gloves had provided some cushion. She twisted her wrists again. The cuff of her gloves moved enough that the rope was now lying against her bare skin.

Providing just enough room to wiggle free.

"What's in those boxes anyway?" She voiced the question to hide her efforts to release her wrists. "If you're going to kill me, you may as well tell me what you're up to."

"I'm not telling you squat," Benton said. "Shut up."

"She saw the boxes?" the nasal voice asked. "Why did you bring her in here?"

Good, more infighting, she thought as she worked against the binds around her wrists. She was almost there. Just a little more . . .

"Shut up already." Benton sounded like a man teetering on the edge. "Or I'll just shoot her now and take you down with her."

"I'm the brains of this outfit," nasal voice shot back. "You wouldn't even be here if not for me!"

Her right hand slipped free. Keeping both arms tucked behind her back, she quickly balled the rope into her left palm so it wouldn't fall to the ground, giving her away.

The light up ahead grew brighter. She still didn't hear any voices, so maybe there weren't additional bad guys up ahead. What if Benton noticed her hands weren't tied once they stepped into the light?

It might be better to take these two down right here and now. She swallowed hard, not liking the thought of taking a life.

Yet she didn't see another option.

Without giving herself time to reconsider, she goaded Benton. "I'm not surprised he's the brains. You've already proven to be dumber than a box of rocks."

He jabbed her in the back again, the way she'd known he would. She stumbled forward, but this time, she purposefully fell to the ground.

Jess rolled to her left, using her right hand to dig into her pocket for the gun. Benton fired first, but his aim went high, the bullet striking the wall a few inches over her head.

Pulling her gun free, she aimed for Benton's center mass and fired. He dropped like a rock, but she didn't wait for his body to hit the ground. She turned to fire at the nasal guy, but he was gone.

It took a second for her to react. Jumping to her feet, she was about to head after him when she heard what sounded like a dog panting.

Whirling, she saw Teddy racing toward her. She dropped to her knees and wrapped her arms around her K9, burying her face in his fur.

"Jess, are you okay?" Logan's voice betrayed his concern. "Are you hit?"

"No, I'm fine." Only by God's grace, Benton's shot had missed. She staggered upright. "We need to hurry. The other guy is getting away."

Logan searched her gaze for a moment, stepped forward, and drew her in for a hug. "I was so worried," he whispered.

She couldn't help hugging him back. Considering she'd about given up any hope of surviving this, she was thrilled to be held in his arms. "Thanks for coming." She forced herself to pull away. "I'm glad you're here, but we need to find that other guy before he gets away."

Logan grimaced and nodded. "Okay. But first . . ." He turned and reached down to check the fallen man's neck for a pulse. He glanced up at her, shook his head, and then reached over to yank the ski mask up to see his face.

She'd killed a man. Nausea churned in her stomach, and it was all she could do not to throw up.

"This is Benton, all right," Logan said. "Or whoever he really is."

She turned away, putting a hand to her roiling

stomach. After a pause, she was able to speak. "I figured as much. Unfortunately, the other guy with a nasal voice was wearing a ski mask, so I have no idea who he is."

Teddy sniffed the dead man, growled for a moment, then backed away, cocking his head to the side as if confused. Teddy wasn't a cadaver K9 like Alexis's dog, Denali, but he seemed to realize Benton was no longer a threat.

"Heel, Teddy." Her dog immediately came over to stand beside her. Taking a deep breath, she lifted her weapon up, holding it with both hands, then moved forward, hugging the wall of the tunnel.

Logan mirrored her movements on the opposite side. When they reached the opening, she was surprised Logan abruptly jumped forward, sweeping his weapon across the room.

Somewhat annoyed, she quickly stepped up beside him. There was no need to be concerned, though. The room was empty.

There was another tunnel leading away from their location. She knew the nasal-voiced man must have taken it. She stared at the dark opening for a long moment.

The guy was probably long gone. Hiding somewhere deep in the labyrinth of the former mine. They could keep chasing him, but he had the advantage of knowing the place better than they did.

She wasn't sure where to go from here.

As if reading her mind, Logan said, "I think we should wait for Doug and the others." He tapped his earpiece, then shook his head. "No radio access down here."

That explained why she hadn't heard anything via the radio since being led away by Benton at gunpoint. She turned to scan the room. It appeared to be set up as a staging area, with several card tables and small kitchen scales, cementing her theory the boxes held components to make synthetic drugs.

As if to prove her point, Teddy sniffed at the closest open box. He sat, let out a sharp bark, and stared up at her.

"You found peppers," she exclaimed. "Good boy." She tossed him the stuffed moose. In her mind, the dog deserved a reward for escaping the bad guys and bringing Logan to the rescue more so than alerting on the drugs. But that was okay. Teddy caught the moose and shook his head from side to side as if playing some imaginary game of tug-of-war.

"Where do you think they're doing the actual manufacturing?" Logan asked.

She waved a hand toward the tunnel. "Guess we'll have to go in farther to find the answer to that."

"Let's turn around and head back," Logan suggested. "Once we're outside, we can come up with a new plan with Doug and the others."

She didn't like knowing the nasal guy had escaped, at least temporarily. But regrouping with the others was a good idea. "Okay. I'm not a fan of tight spaces anyway."

He shot her a surprised look. Then he wrapped his arm around her shoulders and hugged her again. "I'm so glad you're safe."

"Me too." She leaned against him, grateful for the moment.

"Jess, when this is over . . ." Logan's voice trailed off. There was a pause before he said, "I'd like to talk."

About what? She hoped she wasn't reading into his comment as she nodded, then pushed away. "I'd like that. Very much." She cleared her throat and turned toward her K9. "Here, Teddy." She waited for her K9 to bring his stuffed moose back. "Hand."

Teddy regurgitated the moose so that it dropped into her palm. She tucked it away, then stroked her palm over the animal. "You're a very good boy."

Teddy wagged his tail with enthusiasm.

"He found me in the tunnel and made it clear I was to follow him back to rescue you," Logan said as they headed back down the tunnel. Logan used his flashlight to illuminate the way. They had to step around Benton's dead body to continue. "I find it amazing how he can make himself understood without saying a word."

"It's his eyes," she agreed, suddenly feeling weary. The adrenaline that had zipped through her bloodstream while she'd been tied up and fighting for her life had faded fast. "They bore into yours as if he's determined that you'll read his mind."

"Yes. How does he do that?" Logan shook his head. "It's amazing and a little creepy at the same time."

"Teddy is not creepy," she protested. "He's the best dog ever."

"Yes, he is." A smile tugged at the corner of Logan's mouth. "But that stare of his is still unsettling."

Hard to argue that. They walked in silence for a few minutes, Logan playing his flashlight off the walls ahead. She felt certain they were on the right track, but as the minutes ticked by without any sign of the cave opening, a wave of apprehension washed over her.

"Wait." She grabbed the back of Logan's jacket. "I'm not sure we're going the right way. Each of these tunnels looks the same to me. And since I didn't have a flashlight, I didn't notice any of these markings." She waved a hand toward some of the marks and holes in the tunnel walls.

Logan played his light over the cave floor, but

the damp, packed earth didn't reveal any clues. He met her gaze. "Will Teddy lead us out?"

"It's worth a shot." She knelt beside her dog, trying to come up with a way to get him to head outside. "Do you need to get busy? Huh, boy? Get busy."

Teddy stared at her for a moment, then turned to head back the way they'd come. Sensing Logan's concern with Teddy's taking them backward, she shrugged.

At this point, she trusted Teddy's instincts far more than her own.

LOGAN KNEW there were worse things than being lost in an old gold or silver mine, but he was hard-pressed to come up with one at the moment. Maybe because there was still at least one gunman at large.

With the distinct possibility of many more. After seeing the staging area, he was convinced the actual drug manufacturing was being done by others close by.

Yet it was odd that they didn't hear anything, not the murmur of distant voices. Not even the rest of the law enforcement team. He didn't like spending time down here anymore than Jess did.

And really, he'd expected Doug to be there by

now. The plan was to tell the others to find another entrance into the mine and then to come after them. Had something bad happened? He decided not to mention that possibility to Jess. She had enough on her mind. Not least of all being forced to shoot Benton.

Their main concern had to be getting out of this cave alive. From there, they could discuss their next steps. As far as he was concerned, they'd found Benton and the drug stash, so there was no reason to keep Jess and Teddy on the search team.

He'd ask Shane and Doug to send them back to Cody as soon as possible. Granted, that would mean hiking back through the forest, but that had to be safer than sticking around the mine.

When Teddy turned at the next corridor, he frowned. Had they really taken a wrong turn at this Y in the tunnel? As much as the K9's scent tracking impressed him, he wasn't totally convinced the dog would be able to find their way out.

Playing his light down the right side of the tunnel, he could just make out the lump of Benton's body. Seeing the dead guy brought a sense of relief.

They had taken a wrong turn.

"Get busy, Teddy," Jess said encouragingly.

The dog trotted down the other branch of the tunnel. Presumably the correct one that would lead to the outdoors.

Once they reached the room with the boxes, Logan was glad to realize they were on the right track. They crossed through the open space, entering the tunnel on the opposite side. The boxes were evidence, but there was no point in trying to haul them out now.

That was a job for the law enforcement officials.

After walking for a full ten minutes, Teddy lifted his nose to the air. Then his tail began to wag.

Logan cupped his hands around his mouth. "Doug? Doug, are you there? Can you hear me?"

"Logan? Jess?" Doug's voice reverberated off the walls. "Everything okay?"

That wasn't exactly an easy question to answer considering the dead guy lying in the tunnel behind them. He glanced at Jess, who sighed.

"We're not hurt," she answered. "One bad guy is down. The other unfortunately got away."

"Down, how?" Doug asked.

"I—shot him." There was a slight hitch to her voice. "He fired first but missed."

"Good job," Doug said. Yet Logan could tell the accolade didn't make Jess feel any better. She'd need time to come to grips with what had transpired in the tunnel.

Taking a life was never easy. Even when done in self-defense.

Teddy darted ahead, disappearing around a

curve. Alarmed, Logan quickened his pace, only to relax when Teddy returned, his tail wagging again.

A few minutes later, Doug appeared. He hadn't used a flashlight, no doubt unsure of what he was walking into, but Teddy's trusty nose had recognized him.

"It's good to see you." Doug bent to pet Teddy, then enveloped Jess in a one-armed hug. He gave Logan a solemn nod of thanks. "Appreciate your help on this Logan. Care to show me the dead guy?"

"Sure, but where are the others?" Logan peered behind him. "I thought Shane was bringing Bryce to help search?"

"He and Bryce happened to find the other entrance to the mine," Doug explained. "So I told him to stay put until he heard from me. Granted, that was before I realized the radios didn't work down here." He shook his head. "I'm still getting used to operating in the middle of nowhere."

"I get that. Good thing it all worked out." He was just glad Shane and Bryce were okay. Doug too.

Their plan had worked. Granted, it had taken a bad turn when Jess had been forced into the mine by gunpoint, but at least they'd all survived. Logan glanced at Jess who didn't appear thrilled at the idea of returning to the scene of the crime.

But she managed a wan smile. "Yes, I'll take you

back to where I shot Benton. I don't think we have to worry about the nasal-voice guy."

Doug's gaze sharpened at the reference. "You didn't recognize him?"

"He wore a ski mask, like Benton. His voice was lower, raspier and nasal comparatively speaking." She shrugged as they turned to head back the way they'd come. "I'm sure I'll recognize it again when I hear it."

Teddy looked confused for a moment, then fell in beside her. "I'm sure you will," Logan said. He glanced at the dog. "And Teddy might be able to identify him too."

She nodded. "Before the shooting, Benton and Nasal Voice were arguing about their next steps. Nasal Voice wanted to leave everything behind to get out of here. Benton was not willing to leave the product behind. He mentioned they were already behind schedule." She pointed to Logan, then to herself. "Presumably because they took time out to come and look for us."

"I don't like knowing one of them is on the loose," Doug said grimly.

"I know." Jess's voice was subdued. "I feel bad I let him go."

"You were great," Logan said, defensively. "They almost killed you."

"I'm not upset with you or Jessica," Doug said

quickly. "You both did amazing work here today. You're not law enforcement like I am. It'll be my job with help from the game wardens and other officers to track him down."

They walked in silence for several minutes until they reached what he'd dubbed the storage room.

"These are all various components to make synthetic drugs," Jess said. "Based on what I saw in the next room, I'm convinced they're making fentanyl."

Doug let out a low whistle. "There's enough stuff here to make a million dollars' profit, easy. Maybe more."

Ella's face flashed in Logan's mind. He still didn't quite understand why she'd decided to try drugs. Was it something she'd done before without his knowledge? Or had it been her first and last time?

He doubted they'd ever learn the truth about that night.

"Benton is lying outside the next room," Jess said, breaking into his troubled thoughts.

They continued through the tunnel. They all ducked at the spot where the roof lowered. Even Jess.

"There, that's him." Logan played the beam of his flashlight over Benton's body. "I only touched him to feel for a pulse, then to remove his mask." He shrugged. "I probably shouldn't have done that, but I wanted to know who he was."

"It's fine, don't worry about that." Doug quickly covered the distance to reach the dead man. He knelt beside the body, looking at him from all angles. Then he stood and snapped several pictures with his phone.

Lastly, he patted the guy's pockets. The gun he'd used to shoot Jess was lying on the ground not far from his outstretched hand. It took Logan a minute to realize Doug was searching for the guy's ID.

Using his gloved hands, Doug pulled a wallet out of Benton's back pocket. He flipped it open. "Karl with a *K* Matthews. Does that name ring a bell?"

Logan shook his head and glanced at Jess. "Not for me."

"Me either," Jess agreed. "Never heard of him."

Doug grimaced and tucked the wallet into his coat pocket. "Could be another fake ID, but we'll run it through the database anyway." He stood. "Okay, let's get out of here."

"Good." Logan didn't bother to hide his relief. "I'd have never made it as a miner back in the day."

"Me either," Jess agreed.

Doug stood, and together they retraced their steps. Now that they'd taken this route several times, Logan could see where they'd veered off on the wrong path. They turned to take the smaller of the two tunnels, the one where they had to duck to get through to the storage room.

From there, it was another fifteen minutes before he caught the hint of sunlight at the end of the tunnel. Logan had to smile when Jess and Teddy quickened their pace, eager to get out into the fresh air.

He was right behind them.

The minute they emerged from the trees that had partially hidden the cave entrance, Teddy lifted his leg to pee. Logan couldn't help but laugh, knowing the dog had really found the way out just to relieve himself.

"Good boy," Jess praised.

Doug joined them, lifting his hand to his radio. "This is Bridges. I'm with Logan, Jessica, and Teddy. All are safe, do you read me?"

In his ear, Logan heard the various "Roger that" responses.

"One perp is down; there is at least one other at large," Doug said. "Be on the lookout for at least one gunman."

"We've been manning the alternate exit," Shane said. "Nobody has come out this way."

Logan frowned, glancing at Jess. She looked puzzled by that too.

"Are you sure?" Doug asked.

"Absolutely," Shane said without hesitation.

"Bryce and I have been on guard here with Agent Griff Flannery and his colleague. The two game wardens are still out on horseback manning the countryside as are the local cops."

"Okay, thanks." Doug ended the radio transmission.

Before he could say anything more, a voice called, "Bridges? I think I found your guy."

A man emerged from the woods on foot. Logan recognized him as Kevin Tinley, the younger of the two game wardens. Deep in his throat, Teddy began to growl.

Jess grabbed Logan's arm, squeezing it tight enough to be painful. And that's when he knew Kevin Tinley was Nasal Voice.

One of their own had been involved in this drug business the entire time.

15

The game warden was Nasal Voice guy! Squeezing Logan's arm with her left hand to warn him, she slipped her right hand into her coat pocket for her weapon. She was still reeling from shooting Benton, but she wasn't going to let Tinley get away with this.

Teddy's growling grew louder. Her K9 had recognized him too.

"Hey, Kevin." Doug took a step toward him. Just as she was silently screaming a warning in her head, Doug pulled his weapon and held it pointing at the game warden. "Stop right where you are. Put your hands where I can see them. One wrong move and I'll shoot."

How did Doug know he was the other man from

the cave? Had he picked up on Teddy's growling? She froze, not wanting to get in the way.

"Whoa, what's this about?" Kevin pretended to look upset, but he was a terrible actor. With every word, he sounded more and more like the ski-mask guy. Seeing him standing there, she could easily match him with the perp who'd been in the cave.

There must be more than two ways in and out of the mine since Shane and Bryce were standing guard over the one they'd located.

Kevin abruptly dove to the right, hitting the ground and rolling away. She noticed he had his gun in hand, but he was a second too late. Doug fired several rounds, calmly following Kevin's rolling body. Until it stopped moving and the gun dropped from the game warden's hand.

She blinked, stunned. Then she turned toward Doug. "How did you figure out he was involved? Did you pick up on Teddy's growling? I tried to alert Logan, but you weren't within reach."

"Teddy was part of the reason, but also because Kevin wasn't on his horse." Doug crossed over to kick the dropped weapon away, then bent to feel for a pulse. He stood and sighed. "And when you mentioned the nasal voice, I immediately thought of Tinley. He mentioned his broken nose one night when we were working a case. Between Teddy's growling, his nasal voice, and his missing horse, I just knew."

She nodded slowly. "You're one smart guy."

Doug flashed a grin. "Make sure you remind Maya of that."

She couldn't help but laugh. Which was probably what Doug had intended. Her oldest sister, Maya, was head over heels in love with her husband. Their love glowed strong between them. Doug and Maya, as well as Chase and Wynona, had the kind of relationship their parents had shared.

The type of relationship she wanted to have.

Which made her think of Logan.

He slipped his arm around her waist, dredging up a smile. "I knew what you were trying to tell me when you cut off the circulation in my arm. I was reaching for my weapon, but Doug was faster."

"I knew you'd understand." She hugged him back, then frowned. "Two bad guys are down, but we still don't know how many others might be involved."

In the distance, she caught the faint sound of a small plane engine. Lifting her head, she scanned the sky. Their view was limited, due to their standing so close to the side of the mountain. "Logan, do you hear that?"

"Oh yeah." His expression turned grim. "Doug?

We need to get to the airstrip. I think I know who's been helping these guys."

"Big Al?" she asked.

"I believe so, yes," Logan agreed. "Although it could be one of the other charter companies."

Doug nodded and put his hand to his ear. "Game Warden Kevin Tinley was involved but has been neutralized. I need some officers to stay here near the mine while the rest of us head to the airstrip to intercept that plane." Doug looked at Logan as he added, "Logan will lead the way."

"Come, Teddy." She felt bad about not giving her K9 a rest. Teddy gazed up at her, his tail wagging as if to reassure her he was fine.

Doug gestured for them to go first. Rather than heading up the steep incline she'd slid down on her butt, they headed in the same direction Kevin Tinley had come from. As they walked, she swept her gaze over the mountainside, searching for another entrance to the mine.

Burt Jones strode toward them. "You want me to watch the other entrance?"

"Please." Doug clapped him on the back. "Be careful. We didn't see anyone else inside, but we don't know how Kevin got out of there."

Burt looked somber. "Will do."

Logan kept a brisk pace. The sound of the plane engine grew louder now, and as the trees around them thinned, she caught a glimpse of the approaching aircraft.

It was heading in their general direction. And the clearing was large enough to be used as a landing strip. Logan pulled her toward a cluster of trees. "Stay down. It's better if he doesn't see us coming."

She, Teddy, and Doug huddled in the trees beside him. The plane grew larger and larger as it coasted in for a landing. She found herself holding her breath until the bird came to a full stop.

And even then, Logan held back. "There's only one man, the pilot," he whispered. "Which means he's involved."

"Understood," Doug whispered back.

The minute Big Al jumped down from the pilot's seat, Logan shot forward. "Stop! Hands up where I can see them!"

Big Al whirled and tried to jump back into the plane. Without giving herself time to think, she commanded Teddy, "Get him!"

Teddy shot out from the trees directly toward Big Al. The dog grabbed his leg, clamped down tight, and planted all four of his feet, adding his eighty pounds to the effort of holding Big Al back.

Doug and Logan didn't waste a second covering the distance. Doug held his weapon on Big Al as Logan grabbed the guy and tossed him down on the ground. She was impressed, as Big Al had fifty pounds and several inches on Logan.

"Release, Teddy," she said. Her K9 did so, backing away while keeping his dark eyes centered on Big Al.

She stepped forward to envelop Teddy in a hug. "You're a good boy."

Teddy wagged his tail in agreement.

"You're the one who sent Benton a.k.a. Karl Matthews to me, didn't you?" Logan demanded as Doug frisked the guy, finding and tossing a handgun to the side. "You were helping him move drugs all this time!"

"I—don't know what you're talking about," Big Al sputtered.

"Save it," Doug said wearily. "We've already neutralized Kevin Tinley and Benton/Matthews. You're under arrest and have the right to remain silent. Anything you say can and will be used against you in a court of law." Doug continued to issue the Miranda warning, but ended it by adding, "Know that if we find drugs or the components to make drugs on your plane, you are toast. I suggest you cooperate with the investigation or risk serving a life sentence in federal prison. Your choice."

Big Al didn't answer. But the expression in his eyes indicated he might be taking Doug's suggestion to heart.

She turned toward Teddy. "Search! Search for peppers!"

Logan grinned and opened the door of the plane. Teddy went to work sniffing along the ground, then trotting toward the plane. Her K9 gracefully leaped inside, then let out a sharp bark.

Peering into the plane, she saw there were several boxes piled in the back. Teddy was sitting beside them, watching her.

She forced a smile for her K9's sake. "Good boy!" She pulled out the moose, showed it to him, then tossed it away from the plane. Teddy lunged forward, jumping down from the plane and tearing after the stuffed toy.

"Well, well, looks like you're going to be doing time for transporting drugs," Doug said. He grabbed Big Al's cuffed wrists and hauled him to his feet. "Let's go."

"Wait, I'll cooperate!" Big Al said, fear lining his voice. "I'll tell you what I know!"

"Good. We'll talk more once you're assigned a lawyer, but I do need to know one thing." Doug stopped Big Al, forcing the man to look at him. "Is there anyone else within law enforcement involved?"

Jess held her breath again, waiting for Big Al's answer. "Just Kevin Tinley. He made sure no one bothered us here at the mine."

Doug held the cuffed man's gaze for a long moment, then nodded. "Okay then. Let's go."

Teddy trotted to her side with the stuffed moose. She took the toy, then kneeled beside her dog, giving him a long hug. When she stood, Logan caught her close. They stood entwined in each other's arms for a long moment.

Grateful their perilous mission was finally over.

LOGAN DIDN'T WANT to let Jessica go, but when he realized Doug was waiting for them, he forced himself to step back. There was so much he wanted to say, to explain, but this wasn't the best time. He cleared his throat. "I guess we need to head back to the Cabin Creek Campsite."

"Yeah." She went up on her tiptoes and brushed a kiss over his lips. He was surprised and would have pulled her back into his arms, but Teddy wedged himself between them. "Okay, Teddy. We're going."

Doug's voice came through his earpiece as he updated the rest of the group. Before he'd finished speaking, Game Warden Eddie Marsh rode toward them. Right behind him, on Kevin Tinley's horse, rode Sergeant Wayne Carter.

"Big Al?" Eddie's expression was full of disappointment. "What in tarnation were you thinking?"

Big Al bent his head and stared at the ground.

Wayne looked surprised too. "We sent a team into the mine to see if anyone else was hiding in there."

Logan frowned. "The radio doesn't work down there, and cell phones probably don't either."

Wayne nodded. "I know. Now that we know you have everything under control here, we'll head back."

Logan noticed Big Al was looking off to the right. He followed the pilot's gaze. "Wait. If they're bringing their cargo in by plane, there could be another entrance out here."

"Teddy, search! Search for peppers!" Jess commanded.

The dog went to work, sniffing along the ground for a long minute before trotting to the right.

"I'll show you where it is," Big Al said, clearly knowing Teddy would find the opening.

"Teddy, heel," Jess called. "Heel."

Her K9 wheeled from his task and trotted to her side.

Doug pushed Big Al forward. "Show us." The pilot obligingly led the way toward a large rock. Behind it, there were what looked to be two cellar doors. Logan watched as Doug opened them, revealing stairs that led downward.

"Used to be an old homestead here," Big Al explained. "The building fell down, but we discovered the cellar led directly into the mine. We think it was used for bootlegging at one point. It was Matthews's idea to turn it into a drug lab."

"Is anyone else down there?" Doug asked.

The sound of gunfire rang out, answering that question. Doug threw Big Al to the side and headed down the stairs. Logan followed.

The strong scent of chemicals hit them as they hit the bottom of the tunnel. Logan pulled his weapon, trailing Doug as he sprinted down toward the awful smell.

Without warning, Doug came to a stop. When Logan caught up, he gaped in shock. A man was lying on the floor, bleeding from a gunshot wound to his chest. Logan recognized him.

Andrew Tolliver. Their classmate who'd gotten a full ride to Montana State because he was so brilliant in science.

Doug nodded at FBI agent Griff Flannery. "Nice shooting."

"Thanks. He didn't give us a choice. Although he asked if Ethan had sent us, which makes me suspect Ethan Dover's death was no accident." Griff gestured to the weapon that was still sitting on top of the table, next to the Bunsen burners that were cooking some sort of drug combo. Logan was surprised to see that a large generator powered the entire lab. "I didn't dare touch it."

"Agree, nobody should touch anything," Doug said. "We'll need to get a hazmat team here to dismantle this mess. Meanwhile, even a small amount of fentanyl can be deadly, so let's clear out of here."

Logan was only too happy to comply. He turned and retraced his steps to reach the cellar doors, then climbed up to where Jess and Teddy were anxiously waiting.

"It's over for good," he said. "Andy Tolliver is dead."

"Andy?" Jess appeared stunned. "What happened to his full ride to Montana State?"

"No clue." Although he suspected it wasn't an original story. That it was likely Andrew had gotten himself involved in drugs and had decided to use his science skills to make money rather than getting an education and a real job. "Griff said he mentioned Ethan, so I think your theory that Ethan was trying to find the source of the drugs was right. Maybe Ethan ran into Andrew and figured out the connection. Especially since Ella once dated Andy." He jerked his thumb toward the cellar doors. "Based on the sophisticated setup down there, they've been at this for a while. Months for sure, possibly up to a year."

"Well." She let out a long sigh and rested her hand on Teddy's head. "I'm glad we were able to shut them down."

"Me too." He stepped toward her. "Do you think Teddy will mind if I kiss you again?"

A smile bloomed on her face. Then she looked at her dog. "Teddy, lie down." She waited for the K9 to obey, then stepped into his arms.

He kissed her, savoring the moment. Jess kissed him back, giving him hope. While she'd been missing, he'd promised himself that he'd tell her everything. Including the role he'd played in Ella's overdose. Not in the way she'd accused him of, but the fact that he'd broken things off with her.

"We need to talk," he whispered, when they needed to breathe.

"I know." She gazed up at him. "The reason I was so upset after Ella's death was because I had a crush on you."

"What?" He blinked, not expecting that. Then he was struck by even more guilt. "Jess, I need to explain about the night Ella died."

That made her rear backward. "What do you mean?"

"We argued that night. I broke up with her. Told her in no uncertain terms our relationship was over.

I didn't want to see her anymore because I was more attracted to you." He braced himself for her wrath.

"You broke up with Ella?" She looked dazed. "Are you just saying that because I confessed about my crush on you?"

"I'm telling you the truth. I broke up with her that night. She was livid. Called me—well, that doesn't matter. She was upset. Then she overdosed and died." He still felt terrible about how the events had played out all those years ago. "Don't you see? It really is partially my fault. Not the drugs, I swear I knew nothing about her using them. But the reason she'd taken them? Oh yeah. That was totally my fault."

"Oh, Logan." Jess shook her head. "Couples break up all the time, especially in high school. Breaking up doesn't make you responsible. Ella made the decision to use drugs. She didn't deserve to die from her mistake, but it's not your fault."

"Maybe if I had waited . . . or handled it better—"

"No," she quickly cut him off. "Don't blame yourself." She sighed. "If you want to know the truth, my relationship with Ella was strained in those weeks before she died. I think she figured out I had feelings for you."

"Now you're the one just saying that to make me feel better." He couldn't deny her words gave him a thrill. He searched her gaze for a moment. "Did you really have a crush on me?"

"Yeah. A big one." She flushed. "And then Ella died, and I couldn't help thinking you must have known about her drug use. I'm very sorry I lashed out at you in anger. I shouldn't have blamed you."

"I felt responsible." He was being honest about that. From that point forward, he didn't want any secrets between them. "Not because of the drugs, but because I'd broken up with her that night."

"Did Ethan know?" she asked. "About the breakup, not the drugs."

"No, I didn't tell him." He grimaced. "Ethan said some harsh things to me after Ella's passing. I didn't think adding fuel to the fire was smart. Besides, he already blamed me. Giving him yet another reason wouldn't have changed anything."

"You are not responsible for what happened." She kissed him again, sending his heart racing. Then the sounds of Doug and Griff coming out of the cellar doors reached them. Jess stepped back, nearly tripping over Teddy.

He had to laugh at how the dog had gone promptly to sleep.

Doug began issuing orders through the radio. Logan pulled his earpiece out since Doug was standing just a few feet away. Griff did the same thing. Big Al stood with his head down, looking miserable. Logan wanted to rail at him for being so stupid to have gotten involved in drugs, but the man had already made his decision.

Like Ella, Big Al would have to live with the consequences. For now, Logan just wanted his and Jessica's role in this to be over.

They'd done their part. Nearly dying in the process.

After a brief discussion, it was decided that Doug and Griff would escort Big Al to the Cody jail where he'd be held temporarily until they could arrange for him to be transferred to Cheyenne. The local sheriff's deputies and the Cody officers would stand guard at the mine until a hazmat team could be deployed to the area.

Griff had assured them they'd found all the areas that were being used by the drug dealers and that the place was clear. The three dead bodies— Andrew Tolliver, Kevin Tinley, and Matthews/Benton—would have to be taken to Cody as well.

"I'd like to take Jess and Teddy home to the ranch," Logan told Doug.

"That works for me." He nodded to where Shane and Bryce were coming over to join them. "You guys can head back in Shane's SUV. I'll have to stay back to deal with this."

Shane shot him a knowing glance. "I can drop you off along the way," he offered.

"I told Logan he can stay in the guest house," Jess said, before he could agree. "I'll clear it with Anna."

The shocked expression on Shane's face indicated he hadn't anticipated that response. Logan wasn't sure where the guest house was located. He'd been to the ranch five years ago for search and rescue meetings, but not lately other than to pick up members of the family in his plane.

"It's fine, you and Shane can drop me off," Logan said.

"No. I insist," Jess said firmly. "Your place isn't safe until we know for sure all the drug dealers have been arrested." She narrowed her gaze at her brother. "Big Al hasn't been formally interviewed yet. Who knows how many others are out there."

"Fine with me," Shane finally agreed.

Logan was glad to have more time with Jess. And if he were honest, the idea of going to his place alone held no appeal. "Okay, thanks."

They followed Doug, Griff, and Big Al through the woods toward the Cabin Creek Campsite where they'd left their SUVs. Big Al gave his plane a long look as they passed by. Logan knew the pilot was second-guessing his bad choices.

As he should.

Bryce and Teddy ran ahead, playfully chasing each other. Logan fell back with Jess, so they were out of earshot of the others.

"Are you sure about me staying at the ranch?" he asked in a low voice. "Shane didn't seem to like that idea."

"That's just because we don't use the guest cabin very often." She caught his hand with hers. The sun had warmed the air enough that they didn't need to wear their thick gloves. "I'd like you to stay for a few days."

"Really?" He knew he likely looked and sounded like a lovesick pup. "Not just because I might be in danger?"

"I wasn't kidding about that, but the truth is, we haven't had much time to just talk. About ourselves. Our hopes and dreams. Or lives."

"I love you." The words tumbled from his lips. "I told myself if we survived this, I would tell you how I felt. Because we are not guaranteed another day on this earth. And I want to spend every moment from this point forward with you."

"I love you too, Logan." She stopped, turned, and wrapped her arms around him. "As I was fighting to break free of the binds around my wrist, I promised myself I would be honest with you too."

It bothered him to remember how she'd been

captured and forced to kill Benton. He captured her mouth in a long, sweet kiss.

"God was looking out for us," he whispered.

"I know." She kissed him again. "We're very blessed."

"Hey, are you guys going stand there kissing, or are you coming?" Shane called out in exasperation.

"We're coming." He reluctantly pulled away. It was well past time to get off the mountain. But as they continued their hike back to the campground, Logan basked in Jessica's declaration of love.

For the first time in years, he was looking forward to what his future, entwined with hers, held for them.

And he lifted his gaze to the sky to silently thank God for bringing them together.

EPILOGUE

Three weeks later…

Jessica stifled a yawn as she and Teddy headed outside her three-bedroom cabin. She trudged toward the main ranch house, the warm April breeze washing over her. Spring had finally sprung in this part of the state, and she welcomed it with open arms.

Although she could really use some coffee. Anna, the Sullivans' housekeeper, had insisted she attend breakfast with the rest of the family this morning. Jess wasn't sure why since the only day they usually had breakfast together was on Sundays.

Today was Saturday. But since she'd been interviewed by several police agencies, the DEA, the FBI, and even the Cody police chief, she suspected there were still pieces of the puzzle yet to learn. Maybe Doug wanted to give the family an update.

Logan had stayed with them over the weekend after they'd returned from the campground but then had insisted on heading back home. They'd spent as much time together as possible; she and Teddy had tagged along when he'd hiked back out to retrieve his plane. She'd been thrilled that the tail fin they'd found was still with the damaged aircraft. Logan had repaired the plane, then flown her and Teddy back home.

She'd asked Doug to send the plane piece for testing to determine its age and if there was a way to tie it to the one that had crashed with her parents on board. He'd promised to do so, but she knew he was busy tying up the investigation to the massive drug ring they'd busted up.

All thanks to Logan. And Teddy. She smiled as Teddy ran ahead, making circles, grabbing random sticks and darting around like a puppy.

Hearing a plane engine, she stopped and looked up. Then she smiled when she recognized Logan's plane coming in for a landing.

"Come, Teddy!" Her earlier exhaustion vanished as she broke into a run to meet him. "Logan!" She lifted her arm to wave at him.

After landing the plane, he tore off his helmet, jumped down to the ground, then ran toward her.

He swept her into his arms as Teddy barked and jumped on them, eager to participate in the reunion.

Logan kissed her long and deep, then broke off to lavish the dog with attention. "Hey, Teddy. Are you happy to see me too?"

"What are you doing here?" She tucked her hair behind her ear. "I thought you had a charter this weekend and that we weren't meeting until Monday?"

"Change of plans." He took her hand, and together they turned toward the house. "Anna invited me for breakfast."

That much she'd figured out for herself. "Have you spoken to Doug? Does he have more information to share?"

"I have not spoken to Doug recently," Logan said. "Last I heard, they'd made three arrests based on the information Big Al provided. And they found evidence on Ethan's phone that he was taking pictures of Andrew Tolliver, likely because Ethan suspected the guy of being involved. Maybe there's more to add?"

"I'm sure more details will come to light over time." She could be patient. For now.

The rest of the family was already gathered at the main house. Their family gatherings were always chaotic when their nine respective dogs were added to the picture. Chase opened the front door and urged the K9s outside. They didn't mind; playtime was fun.

Anna was in the kitchen. When Jess headed over to offer a hand, Anna shooed her away. "Go. I have it under control. Ten minutes," the older woman added.

Knowing Anna ruled the kitchen like her personal empire, Jess backed out. Wynona and Chase stood with their son, Eli, who was still shy but slowly getting used to being surrounded by so much family. "Hi, Eli."

"Hi." He ducked his head. When Wyn nudged him, he added, "Hi, Auntie Jess."

"I love you, Eli." She dropped a casual kiss on the top of the boy's head. He didn't say anything more, but she knew that any conversation from Eli was a big step for the child.

Doug and Maya were standing close together, speaking in low tones. Jess zeroed in on them. "Care to share what's going on?"

Doug and Maya exchanged a glance. At Maya's nod, Doug stepped forward. The rest of her siblings instinctively gathered around them. "Jessica and Logan, we wanted you to be the first to know that the tail fin you found on the side of the mountain is a match to the make and model of Cessna your parents were in when it crashed. And the age tests that were done indicate the piece was exposed to the elements for at least five years.”

Jess caught her breath. Logan slipped his arm around her in support. “So that really is the likely site where their plane went down.”

“Within a fifty-mile radius, yes,” Maya agreed. “We plan to coordinate more searches of that area. But you have given us a new starting point. And for that, we’re grateful.”

“Cheers for Jessica,” Shane said loudly.

“And Logan,” Justin added.

“When can we start?” Trevor asked.

“Today?” Joel pressed.

“I say we go now,” Alexis said excitedly.

“We’ll create a search grid soon, but I think we have one more announcement,” Doug said. Expecting to hear an update on the case, she was surprised when Logan stepped forward. He turned, faced her, then went down on one knee.

“Jess, will you please do the honor of marrying me?” Logan pulled a small ring box from his pocket. “I love you, and I want nothing more than to spend the rest of my life with you.”

Tears pricked her eyes. “Yes, Logan.” She didn’t bother reaching for the ring. She tugged him up to his feet so she could hug him. “Yes, I’ll marry you!”

“Congrats,” Alexis said, clapping her hands. “That’s so romantic.”

"Another Sullivan wedding," Kendra said on a sigh.

Jess ignored her siblings, focusing on Logan. "I love you."

"I love you too." He picked her up, swung her around, then set her back on her feet. "Chase made me promise to marry you soon, though. He's worried about how much fuel I'm burning flying back and forth."

"Hey, you're the one who asked me for permission to marry her." Chase scowled. "I'm not her father, or Maya's either, but apparently that's a thing these days."

"It's always been the proper way to propose," Kendra pointed out. "And you're the closest thing to a father we have."

Jess turned to hug the youngest Sullivan. "We're doing okay now, though, right? How would you like to help me plan the wedding?"

"I'd like that." Kendra smiled, then hugged Logan too. "Congrats."

Logan took the ring from the box and reached for Jessica's hand. She let him slip the diamond on her finger, pleased at the shine. Then she hugged him.

"Breakfast is ready," Anna said.

She wasn't hungry, but the rest of her family immediately crossed over to the table. Jess hung back for a minute with Logan. "Are you sure you're ready to join this crazy bunch?"

"Oh yeah." He smiled and kissed her again. "I love you so much."

"You fit right in with my family, Logan." Her eyes misted with tears. "Thanks to you, we're going to solve the mystery about what happened to our parents."

"I hope so." He searched her gaze. "But I also hope you don't let that hold you back. Because I really would like to marry you sooner than later."

"I'd like that too." She smiled, knowing her parents wouldn't want any of the Sullivans to forgo their happiness to search for answers.

Every day was a precious gift. She was humbled and grateful to see what the Lord's future held for them.

I HOPE you enjoyed *Scent of Peril*! Are you ready to read Shane and Libby's story in *Scent of Fear*? Click Here!

DEAR READER

Thanks for reading *Scent of Peril*! I hope you enjoyed Jessica and Logan's story. I'm truly having fun with this series. I admire these hardworking K9 dogs, and I hope you like reading about them too.

Don't forget, you can purchase ebooks or audiobooks directly from my website will receive a 15% discount by using the code **LauraScott15.**

I adore hearing from my readers! I can be found through my website at https://www.laurascottbooks.com, via Facebook at https://www.facebook.com/LauraScottBooks, Instagram at https://www.instagram.com/laurascottbooks/, and Twitter https://twitter.com/laurascottbooks. Please take a moment to subscribe to my YouTube channel at youtube.com/@LauraScottBooks-wr1xl?sub_confirmation=1. Also take a moment to sign up for my monthly newsletter to learn about my new book releases! All subscribers receive a free novella not available for purchase on any platform.

Until next time,

Laura Scott

PS Keep reading for a sneak peak of Shane and Libby's story in *Scent of Fear*...

SCENT OF FEAR

Chapter One

Libby Tolliver shifted the bag of groceries in her arms so she could open the door to her grandfather's cabin. "Grandpa? It's Libby."

Her sixty-nine-year-old grandfather wasn't in the kitchen or living room from what she could see. She frowned as she strode to the kitchen to drop the bag of groceries on the counter. "Grandpa?" Her grandfather was usually up and about by now, despite his arthritic hips. She turned and headed down the hallway to the two bedrooms. Her grandfather, Marvin Tolliver, wasn't in the main bedroom, the guest room she used when she came to visit, or the bathroom.

An icy finger of concern snaked down her spine.

Her grandpa wasn't prone to wandering around, but maybe something outside had caught his attention. As it was early June in Wyoming, the weather was mild. She swung open the patio door, then abruptly stopped.

One of two patio chairs was overturned, and there was a broken ceramic mug lying on the ground with a dark stain of what appeared to be spilled coffee. Her heart jumped in her throat as she frantically scanned the backyard.

"Grandpa!" she shouted at the top of her lungs. "Grandpa, it's Libby! Are you okay?"

She didn't see or hear anything. Libby pulled her phone from her pocket and called the Sullivan K9 Search and Rescue Ranch. She'd known Shane Sullivan in high school; he was a year ahead of her. Libby and Shane had never dated. Shane had been seeing a girl named Rebecca Yost, and there had been rumors of a possible engagement. Then Rebecca had died in a terrible car crash, and Shane had taken the loss hard. Especially since it was only a few years later that he'd lost his parents too.

Still, she knew Shane and the rest of his siblings had turned their parents' former glamorous dude ranch into a large K9 search and rescue operation. Libby held herself together with an effort as she waited for the call to go through.

"This is Anna. You've reached the Sullivan K9 Search and Rescue Ranch," a pleasant voice said.

"My name is Libby Tolliver. I'm looking for Shane. We went to high school together. My grandfather, Marvin Tolliver, is missing. He . . ." Her voice faltered for a moment. "It looks like he may have left under duress. Or ran into the woods because he was scared." That didn't sound like her tough-as-nails grandfather, but she couldn't imagine another scenario. "All I know for sure is that he's missing, and I need someone to come search for him."

"I'll send Shane and his K9 Bryce right away," Anna assured her. "What's the address?"

"My grandfather lives a few miles east of Greybull," Libby said, and provided the exact address. "How long will it take for Shane to get here?"

"I'm not sure, but he'll get to your location as soon as possible."

"Okay, thank you." She ended the call, then headed back into the kitchen to put the perishable items she'd purchased in the fridge and freezer before heading back outside to the patio. It occurred to her that she should notify the police.

As she pulled out her phone to make the call, it rang. She quickly answered. "Hello?"

"Libby? It's Shane. I'm halfway between Cody and Greybull and should be there soon. What happened?" Shane's gruff voice helped soothe her nerves.

"I don't know exactly." She stared off at the woods that stretched toward the mountains. "I grocery shop for my grandfather on Saturdays, but he wasn't here when I arrived. One of the patio chairs is lying on its side, and his coffee mug is broken on the concrete." She tried to maintain a positive attitude. "Maybe he saw something amazing and rushed out to get a closer look at it."

"Really?" Shane's voice was thick with doubt.

She tried not to sigh. "I don't know, but I'll head out to start searching. My grandfather has an arthritic hip, so I'm worried he may have fallen. Just get here soon, okay?"

"I will but don't head out yet. Wait for me. Oh, and gather some of your grandfather's recently worn clothing together. Bryce will use them as a scent source."

"I can do that." Libby normally did her grandfather's laundry on Saturdays, too, so she knew there would be a full hamper to choose from. She didn't like the idea of waiting, but it helped her to know he was closer than she'd expected. "Thanks, Shane."

"I'll be there ASAP." He ended the call without saying anything more.

Libby hurried down the hall to her grandpa's room and hauled the hamper of dirty clothes into the living room. Then she headed back outside, giving the patio a wide berth to head toward the woods.

"Grandpa? Grandpa, it's Libby! Can you hear me?" Hearing nothing, she fought to remain calm. If her grandfather had fallen, he might have hit his head and lost consciousness. "Grandpa! We're coming to find you! Don't worry, we'll find you!"

Still no response. Sweeping her gaze over the area, she tried to figure out which path her grandfather had taken. It was a foolish attempt on her part because she had no experience with hunting or tracking. The smart thing to do would have been to wait for Shane and his dog.

Yet she didn't immediately turn back toward the cabin. Realizing she still hadn't called the police, she pulled her phone out again.

But after staring at the screen for a long moment, she tucked the device back into her pocket. Maybe it was better to wait. A tipped-over chair and broken mug didn't really indicate a crime had taken place. Especially way out here in the middle of nowhere. The more she considered that, the less likely she believed he'd been taken away by force. Maybe her grandfather had been startled by something, maybe a bear or some other wild animal, jumped to his feet, and then . . . went to see the animal up close?

She winced. Maybe not. Her grandfather could have simply wandered off. He could have fallen off his chair, broken his cup, and gotten angry with himself, so he'd gone into the woods. Or he'd been confused. She'd noticed his memory wasn't what it used to be.

"Grandpa? Can you hear me?"

The silence was deafening. Libby ran her fingers through her reddish hair and reluctantly turned to head back to the cabin.

After what seemed like forever, she heard the rumble of an approaching car. She hurried out front, watching as a black SUV bounced up the driveway. Shane stopped behind her red pickup truck and slid out from behind the wheel. He was tall and lean, with dark-brown hair and mesmerizing blue eyes. He gave her a nod as the back hatch sprung open, and a huge German shepherd bounded out. Libby took a hasty step backward, fearing the dog would charge toward her.

"Bryce, heel," Shane commanded.

The dog whirled and went straight to Shane's side. The large black and tan dog sat and stared up at him expectantly.

"Good boy," Shane murmured. He raised his gaze to her. "Come closer, Libby. I want Bryce to know you're a friend."

Swallowing against a knot of fear, she crossed

over to join them. Shane reached out for her hand, then brought it toward his dog's snout. "Friend, Bryce. Libby is a friend."

Bryce sniffed her fingers with interest, then gazed at her with his dark-brown eyes. His tail swished over the ground, but up close, the dog was still intimidating. She offered a weak smile. "Good doggy. No biting, okay?"

"Bryce won't bite you." Shane frowned. "Don't tell me you're afraid of dogs?"

"Okay, I won't tell you." She tugged her hand free and stepped back. "Not afraid exactly, just wary. I was bitten by a dog as a kid."

"I'm sorry to hear that, but I promise you don't have to be afraid of Bryce. He won't bite except on my command." As she was wondering how often he'd commanded his dog to bite, Shane turned to head toward the rear hatch of his vehicle. "Let me get Bryce ready and we'll start the search. Do you have your grandfather's clothes?" At her nod, he continued. "If you could place a few items in a plastic bag, that would be good. Dirty socks work well and so do recently worn T-shirts."

Grateful for something to do, she said, "I'll get them."

A few minutes later, she returned to find Bryce wearing a K9 vest strapped around his torso. Shane had a large backpack slung over his shoulders and was chattering with the dog, asking if he was ready to play the search game. Bryce stared up at Shane, his tail wagging with excitement.

"Here." She handed him the bag containing four pairs of her grandfather's dirty socks and a worn T-shirt, trying not to get too close to Bryce.

"Thanks. You mentioned arthritis?" Shane arched a brow. "Any other medical issues I need to know about?"

"He's been a little more forgetful than usual," she admitted. "But he's sixty-nine and will be seventy in November. I figure that's just part of getting older, right?"

"Maybe." Shane was noncommittal. "What's your grandfather's name?"

"Marvin."

"Okay, thanks." He filled a collapsible bowl with water and set it before Bryce. The dog lowered his head, took a few laps of water, then stared up at Shane again. "Good boy, are you ready to search? Here, this is Marvin." Shane opened the bag of clothes. Bryce eagerly buried his snout in the clothing. "Marvin, Bryce. Search! Search for Marvin!"

After one last sniff in the bag, Bryce lifted his nose to the air, then turned and trotted toward the cabin. Shane hurried after his dog. Libby picked up her pace, too, already encouraged by Shane's professional approach to the search.

She was confident Shane and Bryce would find her grandfather. The Sullivans had an amazing reputation for success. Everyone in the area sang their praises. This would work. She refused to consider the alternative.

Hang on, Grandpa! We're coming!

*

Shane was far too aware of Libby beside him. Doing his best to ignore her flowery scent, he gave his K9 Bryce plenty of room to work. He hadn't seen Libby in years, but she looked the same as he remembered. Her auburn hair was wavy and loose, the ends touching her shoulders, and the sprinkling of freckles across her nose made her look as young as she had been back in high school.

She was cute in the girl-next-door kind of way.

Not that he was interested in anything other than finding her grandfather. Just because his oldest siblings were falling in love left and right didn't mean he was joining the club. The girl he'd loved had died years ago. He wasn't interested in trying again.

Pushing thoughts of Libby and Rebecca from his mind, he focused on the mission at hand. At sixty-nine, Marvin Tolliver wasn't that old, but having arthritis meant the guy could have fallen and was right now lying out in the woods, unconscious.

If so, Bryce would find him.

Bryce trotted around the rustic log cabin, not unlike the one Shane lived in on the Sullivan ranch, then abruptly stopped and sniffed intently along the patio near the overturned chair. Shane wasn't surprised when Bryce sat and let out a sharp bark, staring at him.

"Good boy, Bryce." He had Bryce's yellow rubber ducky in his pocket but didn't bring out the reward just yet. This was only the beginning of their game, and he wouldn't reward his K9 until they were further along in the process. "Search! Search for Marvin!"

Bryce eagerly jumped back into the search, sniffing the concrete patio, then trotting out over the grassy lawn toward the woods.

As they followed, he glanced at Libby. "Any idea how long your grandfather has been gone?"

She bit her lip. "Not really. He usually gets up around seven in the morning and eats breakfast, then has his coffee. He sits on the patio when the weather is nice." She glanced at her watch. "It's ten thirty, which means he could have left the patio a few hours ago."

"When's the last time you spoke to him?"

"Last night. I told him I'd be out this morning as usual." She sighed. "I do his grocery shopping every Saturday and then stay long enough to visit while doing his laundry. Grandpa can take care of himself, but I like seeing him each week. I'd drive over more often if I didn't have to work in the hospital billing department Monday through Friday. I've tried to encourage him to move to Cody, but he won't." There was a slight pause, before she added, "After this, I'll have to insist he move in with me. He won't like it, but obviously, he can't stay way out here by himself any longer."

He understood her concern. His attention swung toward Bryce. His K9 was sniffing intently as he moved through the woods, indicating he was hot on the scent. Shane quickened his pace to keep up, unwilling to lose sight of his K9. He and Bryce had been through many searches together. They worked best as a team.

Libby hurried forward too.

"If you need to head back to the cabin, that's fine." He glanced at Libby, then nodded at Bryce. "I'll call you when we find him."

"I'm sticking with you." She sounded a little breathless. "And I appreciate your positive attitude."

He hid a grimace. He wasn't a positive attitude kind of guy. His sisters teased him for his doom-and-gloom approach to life, and he couldn't deny his tendency to expect the worst. But he didn't want to worry Libby any more than she already was. Deep down, he suspected that her grandfather was probably hurt in some way, otherwise he'd have come back to the cabin under his own power.

At this point, the best Shane could hope for was that they found Marvin alive.

Not dead.

He glanced at his watch. During the summer months, they made sure to take frequent water breaks to prevent the dogs from becoming dehydrated. Shane decided they'd walk for twenty minutes before stopping to rest.

"How do you know Bryce is following my grandfather's scent?" Libby asked. "I mean, he just seems to be randomly trotting through the brush."

"Bryce is a good tracker." He had confidence in his dog's ability. "If he lost the trail, he'd stop moving forward, turn around, and come back to the last point he'd located the scent."

"Okay, that helps." Libby's smile was sad. "I pray we find him soon."

Shane nodded, then narrowed his gaze as Bryce abruptly stopped near a fallen tree. His K9 sniffed intently around the log, then sat and let out a sharp bark. Bryce held Shane's gaze as if to say "I found him."

"Is that an alert?" Libby asked, as Shane hurried over to his dog.

Shane scanned the ground beneath the fallen

tree. The dry dirt didn't reveal any footprints, but Bryce had alerted there for a reason.

Had Marvin stopped there to rest? Or had he tripped and fallen? Maybe the old man was confused and managed to get up and continue his wandering path through the woods.

Then his gaze spotted a fuzzy red thread clinging to a spike branch of the fallen log. He glanced at Libby. "Do you have any idea what your grandfather is wearing?"

She looked confused. "Jeans, hiking boots, and a plaid shirt, most likely along with a cowboy hat. Why?"

"What color would his plaid shirt be?" Remembering she hadn't seen him that morning, he added, "Maybe a favorite color?"

"He has plaid shirts in just about every color—blue, green, red, and brown." She frowned. "Not black, though. And no light gray either."

The red thread could have been left by anyone at any time, yet Shane trusted Bryce's alert. "There's a red thread here."

Libby came up to stand beside him. Then she nodded slowly. "I don't remember seeing the red plaid shirt in his laundry basket, so he could be wearing it."

He nodded, then turned his attention to Bryce.

"Good boy!" He pulled the yellow ducky from his pocket and tossed it into the air. "Good boy!"

Bryce ran after the ducky with excitement. He shook his head from side to side as he galloped through the brush. Watching his K9 play with his reward usually made Shane smile.

But he couldn't quite get rid of the niggling sense of concern. The overturned chair and the broken coffee mug indicated he'd been taken by surprise. And that surprise had—what? Caused him to take a walk in the woods?

Could Libby be right about something catching his attention enough to draw him away from the cabin and into the forest?

That theory didn't make sense. Libby's grandfather knew she was coming out to bring him groceries for the week. Marvin wouldn't just decide to take a day hike through the woods without waiting for her.

Unless the old man's memory was worse than Libby had indicated.

"Shane, I don't understand why you're playing with Bryce when we need to keep looking for my grandfather." She looked annoyed.

"I need to reward Bryce for the find; besides, it's time to give him more water." Since they'd already stopped there, Shane shrugged out of his backpack and set it on the ground. He filled the collapsible bowl with water. "Bryce, come."

The dog galloped toward him.

"Hand." Shane held out his hand for the yellow ducky. Bryce obediently regurgitated it into his palm, then lowered his head to lap at the water.

"Wow, that's amazing," Libby murmured, her previous annoyance having dissipated. "I can't believe he just hands over his toys."

"He's a good boy." Shane ruffled Bryce's fur. The dog's tail wagged as if in agreement. He held Bryce's gaze. "Sit." The shepherd lowered his back haunches. "Lie down." Now Bryce lowered the rest of his body so that he was stretched across the ground near the fallen log. "Good boy," he praised again.

Bryce understood this was a rest break. The Sullivan K9s were well trained and had done this often enough that they understood the routine. The only dog that tended to balk at orders was Chase's K9, Rocky.

Rocky's independent streak was a source of amusement for the rest of the siblings, mostly because Chase was the second oldest of the family and accustomed to being in charge. Rocky had a way of humbling their sometimes-bossy brother.

"I wish I understood why Grandpa came this way." Libby's voice interrupted his thoughts. "I wonder if he was following a wounded animal." Her eyes widened. "Maybe he saw a poacher and was determined to get proof to provide to the local game warden."

"Maybe." He figured that theory was slightly better than the idea that the old man had decided to take a hike. "I haven't noticed any animal blood as we moved through the woods, though."

"I wasn't paying attention." She flushed. "I should have thought of that sooner."

"It doesn't matter. Bryce will follow your grandfather's scent, not that of a wounded animal." He stroked a hand over Bryce's fur. "Dogs can distinguish between four million scents. Bryce will know a wild animal is nearby, but he'll stay focused on the search command I've given him."

"Wow." Libby looked at the dog with renewed respect. "That's amazing."

"Yeah." He emptied the water from the collapsible dish and tucked it away. "Ready, Bryce? Search! Search for Marvin!"

Bryce jumped to his feet without hesitation. The K9 sniffed near the fallen log, then began following the scent trail heading in a northeastern direction.

"How much land does your grandfather own?" He scanned the wilderness around them. "I'm just wondering if we'll end up trespassing on someone else's property."

"Grandpa owns about ten acres. The rest is public land. The Bighorn national park is a few miles from here too. That's federal land." She frowned. "It's all a little confusing to me. I guess everyone is supposed to know where the boundaries are located. Grandpa has complained about hunters being on his property, though."

"He's had trouble with the locals trespassing and hunting his land?" He was intrigued by the idea of a poacher or two drawing her grandfather into the woods. Most hunters went out in pairs because an elk was too big for one man to haul out on his own.

Not that June was hunting season for elk or other big game.

"Not recently." Libby shrugged. "The last time he mentioned it was maybe two years ago. And I still think the hunters probably crossed the property line by mistake. Grandpa hasn't put up no hunting signs warning them away, so there's no way they could know they were trespassing."

"Yeah, but hunters are supposed to know where they can and can't hunt. Maybe he did hear a pair of poachers. A gunshot could have startled him enough to drop his coffee." Shane quickened his pace as Bryce followed the scent trail. "Maybe he jumped up, kicking the chair over, to yell at them."

"That could be, but where is he now?" Libby's

wide brown eyes were filled with concern. "Grandpa would answer us if he could."

Shane nodded. "I'm sure he would."

They followed in Bryce's wake for the next ten minutes. They were heading deeper into the woods now, and that was starting to worry him. How far would Marvin go to nab a poacher? Especially if he had arthritis in his hip?

Bryce jumped over a downed tree. The dog liked to run and jump, which meant Shane had to do the same.

"Hurry," he urged Libby. "I don't want to lose him."

"Don't worry. I'm coming." She gamely climbed up and over the log. "Why doesn't your dog take a straight—" Her comment was cut off by the crack of gunfire.

"Down!" Shane grabbed Libby's hand and yanked her down. "Bryce!" His shout was strangled. "Bryce, come!"

His breath froze in his throat as he waited for his K9 to return. The gunfire may prove their theory about poachers drawing her grandfather into the woods, but why would a hunter shoot at them?

Shane had a bad feeling that there was more going on here than Libby's missing grandfather. And he didn't like knowing he, Libby, and Bryce were in danger.